COSMIC EYES

Brian Weinerman

Cosmic Eyes
Copyright © 2023 by Brian Weinerman

All rights reserved. No part of this publication may be reproduced, distributed, or transmitted in any form or by any means, including photocopying, recording, or other electronic or mechanical methods, without the prior written permission of the author, except in the case of brief quotations embodied in critical reviews and certain other non-commercial uses permitted by copyright law.

Tellwell Talent
www.tellwell.ca

ISBN
978-0-2288-9262-5 (Paperback)

TABLE OF CONTENTS

Chapter 1	Memories That Are Not Mine	1
Chapter 2	The Early Part	3
Chapter 3	The Third Presence - The Fetus	5
Chapter 4	The Jerry Host	9
Chapter 5	The Library	38
Chapter 6	Exploration	49
Chapter 7	The Bible	56
Chapter 8	The Wrecking Yard	66
Chapter 9	Abbie Baby	69
Chapter 10	Clinic	79
Chapter 11	The Analyst	90
Chapter 12	A Look At The Past And The Future?	101
Chapter 13	San Francisco	117
Chapter 14	The Communicators	145
Chapter 15	Prescient Or Perverse	176
Chapter 16	Wacky Or Wondrous	184
Chapter 17	The Prophecy	195
Chapter 18	It's Safer In Sacramento	214
Chapter 19	Again, The Newsmakers	227
Chapter 20	Returns	236
Chapter 21	To Unwend Or Rewend	254

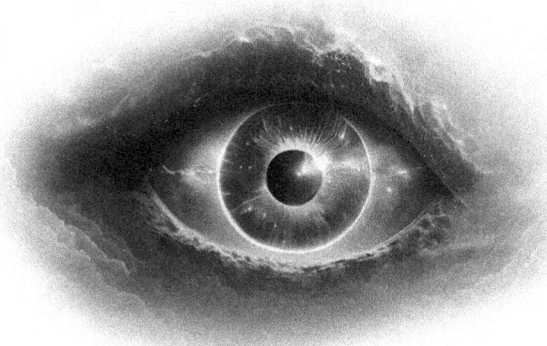

CHAPTER 1

Memories That Are Not Mine

I am old man now—I am talking old, well over a century. The year is 2430, I think. It's hard to remember as I am a little fardrayt (mixed up).

For instance, I am living in a strange cold country. How did we get here, of all places? When I say we, I mean family, friends and followers. Yes, followers, and they were led here by their leader—me! I certainly did not set out to lead anyone anywhere.

But today is a day to talk of memories, many, many memories. My head feels crammed with them. You would expect that in someone over a hundred. But my memories are not like other people's. Sure, I remember growing up in Israel and escaping the Nuclear Disaster to move to the USA. That's normal enough.

What is not normal is the part of my brain that remembers everything in detail, conversations, people, and surroundings. You might think that is wonderful but, although these memories are crystal clear, many of them are not my memories! There are thoughts about events, people or animals I have personally never experienced! These are not my memories! Some of the places I remember, like being in a beehive or running in the forest with wolves, I have not done, at least I don't think. Furthermore, these memories are so damn perfect. I forget what I had for breakfast, but I can play these memories back like a recording. Did I really live as an insect, and a wolf? What about that other family I had in Chicago? I had never been to Chicago. So how can I have a family there? I subsequently went there looking for a child, Ike, and the woman called Helen or Helen Bette. I looked for them because I had died before finishing something with them. But how could I have died when here I am? I really didn't know these people, but I remember them so well, their faces, their smells! Confusing, I know!

Well, let's start.

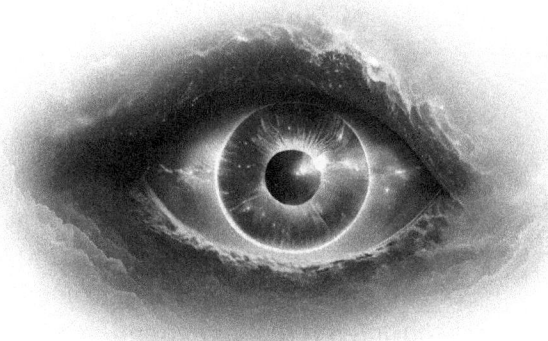

CHAPTER 2

The Early Part

Okay. This part I will summarize because it is kind of boring. I am jumping ahead, but it all started with the feeling of something else in my mind. I am going to give this feeling in my mind a name. I am going to call the feeling the Presence. I never had any physical symptoms of the Presence, but I suddenly had expanded abilities and memories. So many.

In my recorded memory, the one I never experienced, I can call up the feeling like streaming a program, the Presence awoke in the nervous system of an insect, likely a bee. It was looking for signs of sentient beings and realized that this insect was collaborative but not sentient. It directs the bee to a new source of nectar, but on return to the hive, the carrier bee is stung to death by the other bees.

Next, it awakens in another cooperative species, a wolf. Because of the intervention of the Presence, this wolf becomes the leader of the pack and fathers wolf pups, one of which may still have the stamp of the alien Presence.

The wolf stumbles upon a human farmer at the edge of his hunting territory, and the Presence notices that the farmer controls machines. This is sentient behavior. But the farmer naturally is perturbed by the approach of this creature and, after a few visits, shoots the wolf. Despite attempts by the Presence to repair the damage caused by the missile, it cannot, and the wolf dies.

So that was the early time on this planet for the Presence. Now is the time to tell the rest of this story for all those descendants of my followers and whatever family members and friends are left.

I will tell it straight from the recording in my mind, just before they hospitalize me for Alzheimer's or for going looney-tunes. The memories will spill out as if I was living them in real-time, so here goes the streaming of memories.

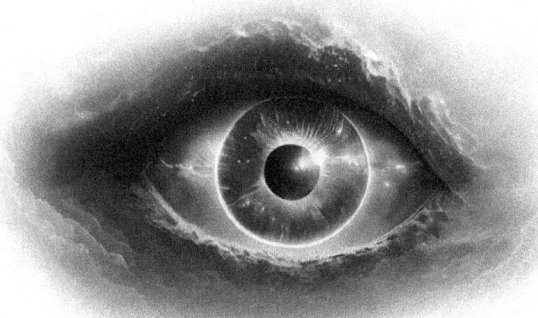

CHAPTER 3

The Third Presence - The Fetus

Awake. This lifeform is at once more complex than the previous beasts and floats in a fluid. It does not appear to be extracting anything from the fluid but receives its energy requirements from a central supply. The creature uses oxygen in its cells for energy. It receives the oxygen from the tube at its center, composed of a system of tubules attached to the inside of the cavity it is floating in.

Unlike the previous host, the oxygen carried by these cells is gathered at the central organ through a complex of vessels separated from another organ by a membrane. The cavity in which this beast lives is in another larger organism that appears to be delivering the oxygen and nutrients at the expense of itself. This creature must be a parasite of some kind. Structurally, however, the bellows, the lungs, exist in this organism but do not appear to be functioning.

It has a two-brained structure, much like the previous creature. This organism app ears to have fewer electrical connections as if it has had few experiences. This creature has little evidence of learning, just the programmed emotions. There may be an opportunity here for us to merge with its mind without doing great damage, as the programming is early. Merge could form this host and easily bend it to the mission. This individual is active, but its movement does not appear to be very purposeful. It does not respond markedly to the environment, but it has a limited environment.

This parasite has no contact with any life form except its host. How does it interact with others of its kind, or does it need to interact to reproduce? There are ovoid structures analogous to that felt in the previous female creature. Therefore, it must contact another of its kind at some time to accept the fertilization as happened with the four-footed creature and mate. Without other contacts, this organism cannot help with the mission. It must leave this host at some time. The organism's structure indicates it must come in contact with others. When will this happen? When will it leave this host?

There is something different about this host. Generally, the cells of this organism are much more active than the previous inhabited. Organs appear to be forming from cell division. The brain structure is dividing as well! Any strengths engraved on the brain would be interrupted by the dividing cells of this brain. This cannot then be a mature organism. This must be an early organism.

This is a developmental stage that will become a mature organism in time. It is kept safe during its developmental stage by its host. This must be a parental host, which is the reason for the nourishment and the reason for the isolation. The organism is in an enclosure awaiting further development in a fluid-filled sac. The host feeds the developing organism. Will this organism develop quickly enough to be useful for what we want to accomplish? Is this the most appropriate type of organism to fulfill the mission? If this organism becomes mature in the future, will it have an influence on the surroundings or on other organisms of its kind?

There is movement! The walls appear to be closing in. The organism does not yet appear to be mature. The lungs are not yet shaped like that of the previous creature. This organism may not be able to successfully extract oxygen from the environment. The organism's central organ now appears to be deficient. The oxygen content of the blood is falling. The host is being expelled through muscular walls, a channel. The amount of oxygen is falling very low. There is death of cells. There is light at the end of a tunnel. The chest muscles are causing expansion of the chest cavity, resulting in the inhalation of the atmospheric air. Extraction of the oxygen is poor. The body is turning a dusky color. The blood supply is cut off from several organs by reflex to protect delivery to the brain, but cells are dying. The heartbeat is erratic and not pushing the oxygenated blood around the body and to the brain. Further brain cells are dying.

This organism is failing! This is not the appropriate time for this organism to enter the outside world!

The lung cells can be made to divide faster, but they need more oxygen. The organism is shuddering, trying to expand its chest but is not seemingly able to accomplish this. The light is fading. The organism is dying. It is happening again as it did with the other organisms!

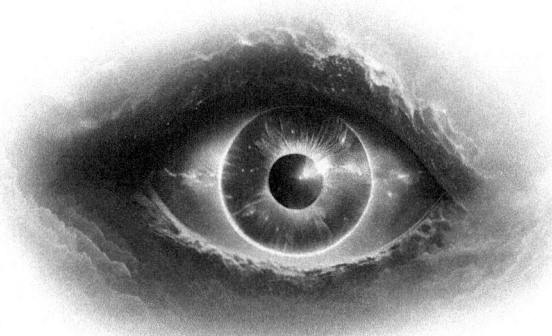

CHAPTER 4

The Jerry Host

Awaken.

This animal is also two-brained, much like the previous being, but much more information is contained on the complex circuit interplay of the brain. This organism has had experience. The connection between the two hemispheres of brain appears proportionately smaller than in the previous brief creature. This indicates a lesser interplay between the two hemispheres. The separation is similar in kind to the forest host, the wolf.

Old Abe breaking in here. I will interrupt to explain to you my streaming service. What I am remembering and voicing is not really in my normal memory. This really is the voice that was within me. I called it the Presence. I will leave it to tell the streaming story.

It is a thinking being, a sentient being. A large area of the brain is devoted to something not related to the senses.

It is located at the frontal area of the brain and was noted in the previous brief creature but was much less developed in the forest creature. This creature is a male and must belong to the same species as the last dead host. But this individual is a developed organism, a mature member of the species. What happened to the previous creature? Why had it left its confines too early in its development? Its survival was made impossible because of its lack of lung function. It was too early in its development, and the lungs were not fully formed enough to extract oxygen from the air. Are we destroying the organisms on this planet?

The mission is important. This present organism is better developed than the previous brief host. The well coursed engrams of instinctual behavior noted in the second host is also present in this host, but many other tracts can be seen. The fibers of these tracts are both efferent and afferent, carrying messages to the brain and leaving the brain, but with a richer interconnection than in the forest host. This host seems more appropriate than the other creatures. It has a greater ability to learn than any of the previous species. The first creature had only long fibers of nervous tissue coursing down through the body.

This host has a sophisticated network, much of it encased in a bony structure coursing down the back of the body, similar to the two previous hosts. This seems to be the main artery of its motor nervous system, transmitting messages to and from the brain. One other major variance in structure from that of the forest host is the area dedicated to the evaluation of scents. The frontal portion of the brain is large, but the region devoted to evaluating airborne odors is not well developed in this creature. The visual color spectrum is enhanced compared to the forest host. This inhabited can appreciate several sharp hews of light reflecting from objects by interpreting the activation of three different cone-like structures in the back of the sensory apparatus, the eye. Only three different cones with varying activation frequencies are present, but by stimulating two or three at the same time, several colors of the spectrum are appreciated by this species. The hues are much brighter than the shades of grey perceived by the four footed one.

The four footed one, the wolf, had not been a good candidate to enable the fulfillment of the mission, but it had been a living being and had been destroyed. At the least, some of its haploid cells were regenerated within the pack. Much would have to be learned to preserve this host and still bring the mission to completion.

"Jerry, you've been standing still and not answering for the last five minutes. What the hells wrong? You having a fit?"

The sound was communicated by a biped standing quite close to the inhabited. This new host is a biped as well. The new host appears to be a similar creature to the one that took the life of the previous inhabited creature—the wolf The biped that killed our four footed wolf was a machine maker and may be the most advanced communicator on the planet.

The large frontal lobe and rich neural net is favorable for this creature, being of the same type as the previous violent one. It must have the ability to manufacture tools and machines. It will be necessary to continue to evaluate this host. This creature may be the correct choice to use for the mission. Finally, a tool-making communicative creature!

Where are we? It appears that we are in an artificial structure.

The outer coverings of this new inhabited are not natural nor like that of the close accompanying biped. The coverings appeared to be a synthetic protection. This was why the creature who had ended the forest host could change its coat. These creatures use protective artificial outer coverings.

The other biped is not carrying any machine or weapon and is smaller than the new host. There does not seem to be any danger from this female creature. The lesson learned from the forest inhabited must be remembered. These creatures can kill quickly without seeming provocation or need to satiate appetite. This is of great concern, but the woman creature does not seem to be a threat.

This creature's consciousness can be controlled, but this limits its activity. It is more difficult in this creature to explore the surroundings without interfering with its normal activities. It plays on its nervous interconnections more than previous creatures. It is necessary to submerge below its conscious level to observe the way the organism carries out its activities without interference. There is no need to submerge immediately since it does not appear that the organism is doing anything purposeful at this time. Further exploration, under full control of its systems, would be useful.

The internal structure of the inhabited is similar to the forest host, although there are some differences in the brain and the protective boney column that house the main signaling and receiving nerve from the brain. This must be a modification due to the present host's upright biped posture.

This host also has a great deal more storage energy in the form of fat laden cells. Most of these cells are centered in the lower half of the main body, causing an outpouching in that area. This host should be able to survive without sustenance for a considerable period of time unless it requires large amounts of energy. It must have long periods of relative dormancy interspersed with periods of intense activity necessitating the stored fat cells. The appendage sacs indicate this is a male of the species.

This host understands in detail the complicated sounds emanating from the other smaller nearby creature. These sounds are becoming louder and more persistent.

"Jerry! What the hells the matter?"

We do not know the sounds, but by tapping into the host's brain, we can interpret the meaning of most of the vocalizations.

Although somewhat smaller than the host, the other vocal creature causing the sound appears similar in structure. There is the hint of two protuberances anteriorly on its body that appear to be different than the structure of this new host. On inspection, these protuberances may also be present on this host but are flatter structures. Small suckling devices (present on the female four-footed creature and used by the little new ones in the former species) are present on this inhabited in the area of the observed protuberances. These suckling devices are not evident in the other animal but may be hidden by the synthetic outer covering. These creatures may use the synthetic outer coating for warmth since they do not have a coat of fur like the lost forest host. The new inhabited has some fur around its face and scattered on its body and around the sacs, but it is not thick enough to effectively keep warm air close to the body. Perhaps it is a survival adaptation to make the present host appear larger and more menacing. The nearby noisy creature does not appear to have the facial fur but has more hair on its head. This could be a sexual difference in this species or simply a variation.

They are in an artificial environment. Light-giving sources are attached to an overhanging structure, and there are at least two apertures with a clear material sealing them, but through which the external planet can be witnessed visually from some height but not sensed by the skin or outer coverings. The host is in a place higher than the main level, and one can see others of the species walking about, along with greenery and bright plants, which the first host was attracted to. There are also machine objects moving about.

The nearby biped is now moving its limbs vigorously in the atmosphere and is also emitting louder sound waves. It has moved to a device that controls the flow of a clear fluid. The creature's molecular sensors do not recognize it in the interplay with the nose nerve endings. The noisy creature turned a tool so that the flow of the liquid abruptly changed from a full narrow stream to that of a slow fluid drip. These creatures do exert control over their environment.

"I'm going to call the medics right now unless you say something."

The noise-producing biped is approaching the host, uttering several louder, possibly threatening sounds, although it holds no combustion machine and is smaller than the new host. There appears to be a mixture of anger, fright, or excitement in the sound wave—something that needs a response. The sounds are complex and varied. They bespeak a communication system built on the production and interpretation of sound waves. We will interpret the sounds through this host's brain. Submerge, to allow the inhabited to interact with the clamorous creature.

"Nothin' wrong, Helen! Shut your face. What's eatin' you?"

"Jerry, you was standing there for I don't know how long and weren't sayin' nothin.'"

"Shaddup, Helen. Where's breakfast? I gotta get goin'."

"Jerry, what the hells got into you? Get your hand outta my fuckin' crotch. You want sex now?!!"

Three smaller bipeds appear, apparently emerging from one of the other compartments. Perhaps they have separate nesting places. One of them resembles the new host but is considerably smaller. One has a similar bearing to that of the vocal biped, and the third resembles both the new larger creatures. The smaller creatures appear to be the young of the species, and in view of the group's close living arrangement and appearance, it is possible that these young are the products of the union of the two bipeds. In our brief exploration, no apparatus was felt that suggested she had a receptacle similar to the female forest creature.

"Hi, Mom, Oh, hi, Dad."

They all utter sounds simultaneously, making it difficult to discern which one of them is actually producing the noise. Their sound wave manifestations are somewhat distinctive, permitting the listener to distinguish which creature is producing the noise.

We are viewing through the Jerry's eyes and hearing through the ear structures.

There are responding sounds from the she biped. They all bend and place the bottom portions of their main bodies, where the lower limbs are attached, on structures that appear suited for the purpose. They are now consuming sustenance using primitive but formed tools, appearing of metal origin. The food they are now consuming is brightly colored and mixed with a white liquid. The brightness of the substance suggests that it might be made of the same plant structures searched for by the first creature. There are other materials to eat which are placed on another higher structure upon which they place portions of their upper limbs. There does not seem to be the excitement or quarreling in their eating patterns, as previously displayed by the forest host, the wolf and his pack.

The new inhabited did not appear to try to initiate sound communication to the same extent as the others. Hostility and anger seem to be emerging on the right side of the brain, not dulled by any other moderating electrical impulse waves from the left side or the frontal portion of the brain. This interpretation is justified since similar molecular reactions were noted previously in the former host when fighting with the pack leader. However, presently, no definite threat is evident. The cause of these hostile reactions in this new host is unknown. They are apparently coming from stored memories and are being activated again by the sight of this group of bipeds. Why these bipeds provoke such a violent response, although appearing poorly equipped to threaten, is not apparent. There is no obvious danger from an enemy or any of the bipeds present, but memories of other encounters with other bipeds seemed to be being replayed on the right brain, feeding the rage reaction. There seems to be a curious imbalance, great rage, but a lack of realistic modification from the left or suppression from the frontal area. These areas operated more smoothly in the forest host, although the frontal area was considerably smaller.

The host is now going through the same motions as the small bipeds, bending itself and sitting. He starts drinking a liquid, surprisingly hot and damaging to the epithelial layer of membrane in the mouth. He does not appear to note the reaction despite the impulses travelling from pain fibers. He begins eating some of the food placed on the raised structure.

The sustenance can be evaluated through the nose by an interaction with the molecules carried in the air sending messages to the brain. The food seemed to be composed of animal matter somewhat akin to the flesh of the large forest kill.

"Bye, so long, see ya."

That sound was expressed by one of the three young. Two of the young leave their sitting structures which are called chairs by the woman figure, and depart from the enclosure through an aperture. The opening was not previously apparent and was only produced when one of the young turned a device and pulled out a portion of one of the side sheets constructed to compartmentalize the dwelling.

"Jerry, today is payday, and we need the money real bad, so don' go drinkin' it away tonight with the guys. The kids need some clothes 'cause winter's comin."

The inhabited swings one anterior limb impacting it on the front orifice and sensor apparatus of the she biped. The rage in the brain had flared at the sound waves the she biped had discharged. The area of his brain now activated was most pronounced on the right side of the bilobed organ.

Surely the female creature would not be receptive to his wish to pass along his information packets after such a blow that appears unprovoked. One possibility is that the transmission occurs when the she animal is unconscious. It would seem then there would have to be some other bond between male and female as surely the attack would be avoided by the female. That could result in difficulty in replicating the species. By the number of dwellings evident, and there appear to be many large structures in the area similar to the one in which we find ourselves, this species is successful at reproducing. This may be an aberrant grouping, although they have successfully acquired progeny.

The host is now tensing a lower limb muscle and may be about to use one of the lower limbs to strike out at the female biped. The female is in a prone and defenseless position on the floor. It seems without worth to kill the female. Although this is now interfering with their reactions it seems reasonable and necessary to quell the rage in the host immediately. This reaction must be properly assessed and understood.

A small charge to the rage area will result in a pain sensation in this male and stop the action by interrupting the rage current. Another electrical circuit was now established.

"Leave her alone, you shit, or I'll kill ya," were the sounds originating from the small one resembling the host. It positions itself between the fallen female biped and the Jerry.

Submerge to watch the reactions of the inhabited after the electrical modulation. By submerging, we allow the Jerry to control himself. What will his reactions be after this violent exchange?

"I'm sorry, Helen, Ike. Don't know what got into me. Gotta go to work now, anyhow."

The Jerry stands there, seemingly unsure, and shakes his head after the electrical charge.

"Asshole, remember, don't drink up the money! You shithead. You know I can't work now, and my subsidy just all goes for the rent."

The Jerry makes a motion with his upper limb as the female rises. The Jerry leaves through the aperture that the small female had used. He is now in another compartment, a large narrow enclosure, and descends through a passageway approximately four of the Jerry's height. The passageway was constructed of many small tree cell platforms, each slightly lower than the other, enabling the bipeds to ascend or descend.

The host emerges from the enclosure using a similar method to develop an aperture as he previously performed. Outside the enclosure is the flat rock surface noted previously through the clear sidewalls. The surface is made on two levels. The outer slightly raised, narrower flat surface is filled with bipeds, and the more central area is filled with various moving large machine objects. The machines appear to be composed of artificial, brightly colored solid materials. Many of these machines are intermittently attached to a metallic-looking band raised slightly above the flat surface. At least two bands are running along the wider flat surface.

The large machine devices are surely manufactured from artificial substances and are directed by the biped race. Jerry, the host, moves on the raised flat to an area where descent is possible via platforms made of metal rather than from forest material, but similar to the one he had used to emerge from the previous enclosure.

The bipeds are numerous here. Many of them produce sound waves, so there is a steady background hum. The mechanical vehicles are largely silent but occasionally make loud noises,

The outer artificial coverings of the bipeds are all different in color and shape, although there is a symmetry to some of the coverings worn. There were both complementary types of bipeds, although they displayed a few different skin hues or shades on their upper bodies, heads, and faces. The complementary ones are called men and women (on exploration of the Jerry brain).

The perception of the spectrum of light in this species is far greater than was present in the forest host but not in the other former species. The sense of detecting molecules in the air by the anterior sensory apparatus—the nose—is more poorly developed than the former forest host. This could be strengthened in this host and even changed in the haploid of the Jerry if it were to have survival value. This could also be a gift. A small amount of increase in the correct neural pathway would allow a heightened perception of incoming molecules despite the small portion of the brain devoted to this activity. Surprisingly, the brain is larger than in the wolf, but so little is devoted to the smell sensory area.

This change is done. It will be observed for benefit and then implanted in the haploid cells.

The Jerry stepped on a structure which was also a biped controlled device running on a flat metallic structure with holes at frequent intervals. These seem to be pressurized with atmospheric gases several times the environmental pressure. This allowed the moving structure to rise above the metal and propel itself with little friction, although a portion of the device always touched the metallic band. It is probable that an energy supply came from this structure.

The Jerry stood as the machine started moving and stepped off after the device stopped and started four times.

We are ascending the step platforms similar to the one previously descended and are proceeding on the flat area rich with other bipeds. There is very little acknowledgement or exchange between all these creatures. This is very different than in the group of wolves we experienced. These bipeds seem not to sense one another, although the signals are being received by all the sensory apparatuses. The Jerry now enters another rock-side dwelling the Jerry calls a factory. This is noted by others voicing the factory sound. The large mixture of smell molecules is immediately sensed by the newly heightened smell center, and the host reacts by forcing air through the anterior organ, the nose. The Jerry does not seem pleased with the new ability to detect scents. The reception and increased awareness of the scents noted in the factory seem to have a different effect on this host when compared to the enjoyment experienced with this faculty by the former forest species.

When the smell was noted by the former host, the molecules were evaluated, the direction determined, and the likely source catalogued against the stored memories. An image on the brain of the smell source was formed if the smell had been previously encountered. The Jerry does not savor the odors or make any use of the information other than to try to dismiss the odors from the nose and the brain. The strong sense of the smell seems to make this Jerry creature unsteady as it attempts to climb the steps of the factory dwelling. A few electrical charges moderated the new smell sensation, and the creature seemed to have recovered his equilibrium.

"Jerry, you're late again! If you want to keep this job, you'd better smarten up. It won't be good for your wife and kids or your parole officer. Now keep your fucking cool, and don't try to give me any of your lip!"

"Okay, Sam."

Cosmic Eyes

The rage reaction had flared very slightly, but the short rage circuit had been interrupted. The Jerry now seemed to be able to allow other sensations to touch him and moderate the brain rage area. The Sam biped appeared somewhat surprised at the muted response received from the Jerry.

"Now get over there to Zep, and he'll give you your assignment today."

The host moves to the area of the compartment occupied by the biped Zep.

"We're making hide-a-beds today cause I guess we got an order. You know we sell these as handcrafted, not machine-made. Have not made these things for a long time. It's amazing we are making them here again. You can tell Helen later that they'll need some piece work for the coverins so she can pick up some extra scratch. These are the three pillow jobs, and we need fifty. The frames are over there. There are the right sides, left sides, backs and springs. You can figure out how to assemble them. The pins and drivers are over by the window. Call if you need help. I'm going to work on the frames. Load the assembly on the conveyer, taking them to the coverin' area. Remember, we got to do this good 'cause it has been forever since we made these things in Chicago."

We are not sure as to what the Jerry is being asked. We will submerge since the Jerry seems to know what to do and what is to be made.

Jerry started to assemble the hid-a-beds. After apparently completing the task, he then placed the product on a low, slow moving flat device that bore the object to some other compartment in the dwelling place factory. It is a slow process. Lining all the assorted parts in their correct alignment and working up one side and down the other should increase the speed at which these primitive machines could be produced. It also meant the tightening of the metal attachments which bound the objects together could be done all one way and then the other without so often changing the tool. Perhaps they did not wish to make many of these machines as the usefulness of these primitive devices is not apparent.

"Coffee and donuts at Sal's, Jerry. Come on; you're usually the first one off the mark. What's wrong with you today?"

The host started to accompany the Zep. It was obvious, on exploration of the meaning of the sounds, that the Sal was a place. It was not immediately obvious why the bipeds were attending this Sal place, but it may be for the gathering caloric sustenance as the Jerry has signals coming from the food tract, indicating hunger. Although the host brain circuitry indicated its wish to go, there seemed no obvious immediate need in view of the large energy stores present. A mild charge deflected the initial acceptance, as the project to which the host had been assigned was just getting underway.

"No, I'm gonna work on these hide-a-beds."

"You kiddin' me. Jer?"

Merge.

"No, there is much work to be done before my task will be accomplished.

"Shit, okay, suit yerself. You're lookin' a little different today, Jer. Hmm, bye for now."

There is not the space necessary to align all the components, but many can be done at once. We will begin the task. The most effective way will be to bring together all similar component parts. Now they can be assembled. The assembled hid-a-beds can now be placed on the moving machine. This machine apparently carries the hid-a-beds for placement of other spring parts and something which is called coverings. The new process is much more efficient.

The Zep is sensed approaching. It is an easy task to recognize the individual smells of the bipeds. Their scents are more distinctive, sharp, and not pleasing. They differ from that of the members of the pack. Changes in emotion are easily detected in others, with the ability to slightly modulate and heighten the awareness of the smell. It is necessary to dampen this awareness even for the comparatively small center which examines the incoming scents. Too much sensitivity seems to cause other sensations in the Jerry. Too much smell causes stimulation of another center, and activation of this causes reverse peristalsis of the upper intestinal tract. This might lead to the elimination of the nutritional sustenance he had ingested in the Helen dwelling. The increased perception of the smell organ, the nose, may not be an advantage to this species.

"Jer, ya comin'for lunch or are ya even goin' to work through chow time?"

"It would seem reasonable to ingest something Zep, as I have a grinding sensation in the upper intestine and visual sensations flashing in the brain."

"Jeezez kerist! You have flipped."

Despite the large store of energy carried by the Jerry, it was apparent that it was necessary to constantly take in energy, as the body was attuned to it. The brain certainly seemed to desire it and enjoyed the thought of the food. There appeared to be some damage to the organs of the body, secondary to this over-ingestion pattern. Fat deposits swelled the fat-containing cells, especially around the middle of the body and on the inner aspect of the channels carrying the oxygen-carrying cells in the fluid. Some of the channels had a reaction around the fat, so the channels caused turbulence of the fluid, the blood. It was conceivable that if these fatty deposits build up to a great extent, they may actually stem the flow of blood to a portion of the body and do untold damage. This would have to be examined later, and the mechanism for removing the occlusive substances discovered. The substances reacted with enzymes and small nucleus-free cells in the blood to develop a partial occlusion of the vessels.

One of the organs in the abdomen, under the bellows, the diaphragm, appeared also to be filled with fat.

"Jer, are you okay? What's eating you today? Are you comin' or what?"

Submerge.

"Sure, I feel hunger and should eat something."

Jerry moves with some of the other men and women who work in the factory. They move out of the factory and down the platforms to the street, where they enter another flat-walled structure, a building. This building apparently has a name, Sal's. They all entered and picked up flat nonorganic-looking thin flat objects which were pushed along a metal-appearing projection. On one side of the projection was an array of possible consumables, already killed or plucked, changed and packaged to render them edible. Some obvious foliage was present under a transparent partial enclosure. The foliage could be readily accessed. It was reasonable for the Jerry to partake in this act and consume this as sustenance. There are many sounds; the bipeds are emitting some, the bipeds serving food, the sliding along the metal projections. It is a profusion of noise compared to the forest.

"Anything else for you, sir? Your usual burger and large fries?"

"Of what is this composed?"

A woman with a white cap and dressed in a white covering is making these sounds and appears confused as she is partially closing her eyes.

"You mean the burger? Is that a joke?"

"I do not understand the reference. Of what are they composed? Do they contain much in the way of energy provision? Is this the best substance to eat?"

"Are you puttin' me on? Look, I'm busy. This is what you have every single day."

It is evidently necessary to completely submerge to allow the Jerry to function in a manner representative of his species. If not, they may all turn on him and end his life, as happened to the first species. A complete submergence is necessary so as not to cause suspicion of the surrounding group.

"So, what will it be?"

"Burger and large fries, extra ketchup.

"Seven-fifty in credits."

"Oh, yeh, take the credits off this and add 25. Now hurry with that stuff."

"Hurry? You stood arguing for 10 minutes. You're really acting strange."

The rage reaction flared again but did not feed on itself with the altered reaction status in place. A charge moved the Jerry toward the others perched around a flat platform and ingesting quickly.

"What's all the fuss about, Jer?"

"Nothin'. She didn't hear me order the burger or somethin', and she got all riled up."

"Is that all you're gonna eat? Just that salad?"

"No, the burgers comin' although I'm not that hungry today, and the salad looks sorta good. Maybe I won't have the burger. I could afford to lose some fatty tissue."

"Strange, Jer, strange. I never seen you eat salad."

"Well, it's payday today. Is anyone going to the Sherbrook after work? Jer, I know you'll make it."

"Yeh, I guess so?"

"Time to go back to the sweatshop."

The reverse route is followed on the return to the factory. The Jerry will now put the plan back into effect.

The Zep is now calling again for a coffee. A coffee, apparently, is not necessary for the Jerry to attend or ingest.

"What are you doing, Jer? It's a TGIF payday and quitting time. Let's hit the Sherbrook."

SUBMERGE.

"Jerry, here's your credits. What happened to you today? You sure are acting strange. Do you know how many you framed today?"

"I believe so."

"Well, I don't have the count, but the spring fitters were saying that the conveyer belt just kept coming, so they had to start piling them up. They never saw you work so fast. Did Zep tell you to tell Helen that we will need some compusewing done? She's said she wanted the piecework, and I got nobody on our compusewer right now, so make sure ya tell her.

"Yeh, I will."

"Okay, have a good weekend, and good work today. I really appreciate it."

There appears to be a surprise in this person in the production of the Jerry today. There was some rage reaction in the Jerry, indicating some tension, but this is easily stopped.

"Thanks, bye. I didn't know I put that many frames together today. I was kinda in a fog, like sleepwalking, and then I woke up, and it was quittin' time."

"Well, you maybe should do more sleeping like that more often. Bye!"

The Jerry is now almost alone in the large factory. The other creatures have left or are leaving. Submerge. The Jerry now also leaves the factory and moves down the platform, and walks toward another enclosure, a building. This is not a building that has been previously entered that day, but he sees the other workers entering. He pushes on a see-through entranceway door. The see-through door yields to his push, and the Jerry enters the new building. There are many bipeds present here. Many are sitting at a long, raised platform behind which stand other bipeds. The bipeds standing behind the platform pour liquid almost exclusively and give the liquids to the seated bipeds. It appeared that they were also exchanging the credits that the Jerry had used at the Sal's. The Jerry moves forward and also requests a liquid from the biped, the bartender.

"Take the credits. I got plenty today and take an extra 20 for you."

"Okey, dokey."

The Jerry picks up the obtained liquid material, drinks a portion of the liquid, takes the liquid container in his hand outer covering, and leaves that room of the building to go to another portion of the enclosure. As he approaches the door, his body breaks a beam of light. This apparently serves to activate a circuit through electromagnetics. The force of the magnet can be felt. The circuit created drives a small motor, allowing the door to open without direct contact by the bipeds. The light beam is contacted, but the door does not open for the Jerry. This is curious, but since Jerry is radiating energy now because of our presence, we must be keeping the link intact. The host, in fact, cannot be detected by the light beam since we are replacing that energy. Direct physical contact and force will be needed to enter the new space through the door.

"What the hell's wrong with this door?"

The Jerry uses physical force to slide the door into a recess in the side of the building.

"Jer, we're over here. We've already done our first round, so you can buy the next."

Jerry swallowed the liquid he had obtained for the credits by raising the container high above his lips and letting the liquid reach his mouth from a height. This was not the same liquid, a combination of hydrogen and oxygen, that the previous host had lapped in the forest and which was present in much of the body of this and the other four-limbed forest beings. This liquid contains a substance that reacts with some brain receptors. It is bitter. The substance has the effect of lessening the input from some of the centers in the frontal portion of the brain and allowing other functions to progress without as much interruption. It also seemed to activate the sleep center and cause some fatigue in the host. Synapse times are somewhat slowed. Directions from the left-brain side are somewhat inhibited, allowing the right side to act more independently. It is a way of modulating brain function and taking away some of the supervisory control. In the case of the Jerry, the rage reaction was not quite as suppressed as previously, even with the inhibitory program in place. This may not be desirable in this individual if we are to pursue the course that is needed.

Re-emerge and control the Jerry.

"I have some important things to do, and the liquid has changed my controls. Therefore, it is necessary now that I leave."

"What! You just got here, Jer. You owe us the next round!"

A slight charge is all that is necessary to make the Jerry start moving to the self-opening see-through door. Since the ingestion of the liquid, the actions were simpler to control.

"The ball and chain. Told ya. Had to be home early? Jer, are ya becoming a wimp?"

"Shaddup, Tim! Jer doesn't seem hisself today and don't get him riled. You know he starts cracking heads with that temper of his."

"Well, he don't seem so scary right now!"

A strong molecular sensation is present and detected by the enhanced neural mechanism supporting the nose. The smell of the Tim has changed and is becoming stronger, much nearer. The detection of this and the change in the scent touches off the same type of reaction as the menacing gestures of the leader in the previous wolf pack. The Tim must be approaching from the back of the Jerry. It is, therefore, necessary for the Jerry to remove himself from the path of the Tim biped. The Jerry neck is exposed, so a lateral movement is necessary to protect the vital area. This is performed. The move causes the Tim to pass the side of the Jerry, as the rapid alteration in the progress of the Jerry seems to have surprised the Tim. He is not nearly as quick as the forest pack leader. His neck is exposed, but it may not be necessary to kill the Tim animal as he does not seem agile and, therefore, not dangerous. He does not seem to be carrying any destructive machine of metal. His aggressive manner may have resulted from the intake of the special liquid. It is interesting that this species could have survived when they further inhibited their rather slow reaction time with the ingestion of these materials. The substance itself may lead to aggression. The development of technology must have occurred before these habits. Otherwise, they would not have prospered as they seem to have.

The Tim tries to turn but is not balanced and almost falls. A gentle push from the Jerry inhibits the Tim from regaining balance, and he is on the floor. The rage reaction in the Jerry flares at the sight of the helpless Tim but is modulated so as not to further injure the Tim. The Tim does not seem to present further threat now. I must push the Jerry to continue. Killing the Tim would seem unnecessary and did not really seem to be imaged in the Jerry's mind, although the anger there would have caused further injury to the Tim. It is unlikely that the lack of killing the Tim will be looked upon by the other bipeds as unusual. Killing was not in the mind of the Jerry and therefore improbable to be foremost in the other minds.

Jerry approaches the see-through door. He again uses force to open it. The Jerry descends into the underground area. This is the area he had ascended from previously at the beginning of the day. He now retraces his earlier steps and returns to the dwelling place, the home of the Helen.

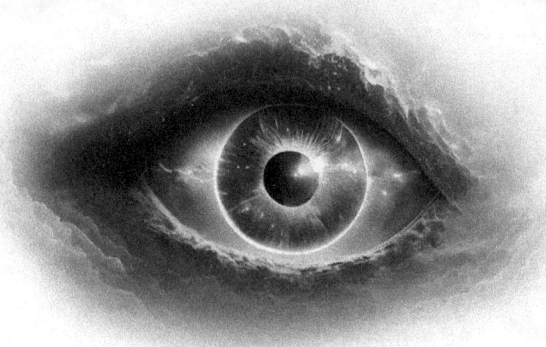

CHAPTER 5
The Library

The Jerry enters a machine, which many bipeds are riding in.

The hanging, moving machine rides quietly on the pressured carpet of air. The carbon metallic structure apparently was designed to allow little friction to take place. No attempt was made to use the heat generated from the friction from the hanger-like apparatus. It was wasted to the atmosphere. The machine came to a halt.

Submerge so that the Jerry can find the correct departing place from the moving machine. As we let go control, the Jerry experiences flares of electrical brain activity, almost compelling him to return to the place of the Tim. These brain activities are readily quelled by small manipulations. The artificial substance which carried the credits is sensed by the fingertips in the artificial covering. The sensation again makes the Jerry again wish to return to the place of the glass doors. It is the paralyzing liquid that the brain of the Jerry, with receptors now empty, seems to demand! We need to create again the electrical discharges in the brain which coerce the Jerry to reverse his direction . . . merge.

We must now control the impulses and the anger of the left brain of the Jerry. The interplay of the two brains under normal circumstances does not seem to be enough to moderate the anger responses in this host. We must allow the Jerry enough memory to operate and find the Helen home. A change in his direction and return to the place of the platform and the liquid will not be permitted.

The Jerry now approaches the home, mounts the fixed platforms, and tries the dwelling door. It will not respond to his attempts to open it. There does not seem to be the necessity here to break a light beam or anything requiring energy. When he left previously, the action was a simple mechanical one. The Jerry reaches into his covering and withdraws a metallic device, placing it in an aperture in the door. There is still no movement in the entranceway, even with the application of force. Submerge to permit the Jerry to understand the cause of the problem. The difficulty is investigated in the brain of the Jerry. The explanation for the hindrance is now apparently evident. He is banging on the door with his knotted fists.

"Hey, let me in. It's Jerry!"

"I phoned your work. You didn't come home right after work, you asshole. You went to the Sherbrook.

Probably the only reason you're home now is that you lost all the credits on some type of stupid bet! We talked about this. Jerry, we needed the money. I told you I wasn't going to take it anymore. But you do it every time, no matter what. How can you come home broke and drunk again!"

The rage reaction flares in the Jerry. Complete merge is always necessary in this destructive animal to control the reaction. Credits are represented by the plastic in the pocket but most likely remain intact. There was the wish to return, and this was linked to the sensation of the credits.

"The credits are approximately in place. No great loss was experienced at the Sherbrook except for the purchase of a single mind-depressing liquid. close to the amount given."

"Wow! You have never done that before! Jerry, you sound so strange again but not drunk. Ya mean ya didn't go out with the boys? They said at the shop you went with Jim and Tim. They always go there."

"I did enter the Sherbrook but only had one glass of the liquid, for which credits were given. That amount is no longer present on the card. It would not be likely that the card would now be worthless."

"Jerry, you sound really strange. You look like yourself on the addressor. Are you okay? If I let ya in, promise ya won't wallop me?"

The flare reaction is again there. The anger is present. The electrical discharges are actively suppressed by the covering activity of the merge. A reworking of the brain in an area of the cortex will be necessary to let the Jerry emerge from control, and yet ensure that the peculiar aggressive reaction will not appear. This is changing the Jerry creature more than any of the other creatures, but these anger reactions do not appear to benefit the Jerry in any way. He cannot be left on his own. We need a great deal of control on the Jerry; he cannot act for long on his own.

"There will be no aggression. Allow me to come in."

"Okay, Jerry. I'll open the door, but if you try anything, I'll scream bloody murder. If you beat me up again, I'll get you, I swear. I don't care if they throw you back in lockup and throw away the key."

The door opens, and the Helen is seen holding an instrument. There is a smell to the metal object, much like that of the instrument, which resulted in the kill of the forest creature, the wolf. This display of a killing object by the Helen was not matched by ferocity in her manner, but her expression is one of fear and not aggression. We must not allow the Jerry to be killed, as his normal reactions are paralyzed.

At this time, the merge is keeping the Jerry brain tranquil. The Helen can be overpowered, as the Jerry is larger and certainly stronger from a physical point of view. This would mean another killing or rendering of harm. Is there another way to diffuse the situation without exposing the Jerry to harm? Supplication does not always seem to guarantee survival or freedom from reprisal with these bipeds. She wishes the credits. We will cause the Jerry to produce the card that contains the credits.

The Jerry reaches into the covering and gives the credits card to the Helen. The facial features of the Helen change; the wrinkle in her upper face disappears, her eyes are no longer narrowed, and her mouth appears to show teeth but not in an aggressive manner. The instrument is lowered. The situation appears to be improved.

"Jerry, you really did bring the pay home! I was so hoping you would, even though somehow I was set for not believing it. I wasn't going to take it anymore, Jer, I wasn't. This will make all the difference. Come in, and I'll get supper on the table. Thanks, Jerry, thank you!"

Suddenly, the Helen reaches up and presses the forward orifice, the mouth, to the similar orifice of the Jerry. The Jerry notes the sensation as pleasant, no fear or anger. The rage was naturally quelled. Several other neuronal pathways are initiated in the brain, and peripheral neuronal discharges are occurring. These reactions cause an engorgement of the projection between the legs. Submerge and allow the Jerry to act again by himself since the rage has now been quelled. The Jerry makes a movement with both his arms to pull the Helen toward him, but she gently pulls away.

"I feel like it, Jer, but the kids are home, and I want to put on supper."

"Hi, Dad. How do you do? I'm a gnu, and I'd like to gnash my teeth at you."

"Ike, shaddap! You'll get your dad mad again."

"What is a gnu?"

"I don't know, dummy Dad. It must be on the net. Google it."

There are no memory tracings in the brain of the Jerry that refers to a gnu or to a gnash. It is not known what a Google is.

"Is there a place where I can see all the words of the language we speak?"

"You're kidding, Dad. You're not mad at me? I didn't even know you could read!"

The rage reaction flares slightly. We must keep control of the Jerry in order to progress. He does seem unable to carry on a discourse with members of his own pack without rage flaring.

"I can read, Ike. Do we have what I have asked for?"

"Uh, I have a small old dictionary that came with the used Solitaire game we got. I guess there's a big one in the library. But you could do it all online."

"I might have some difficulty using the online machine. Where is the library? Can you take me to it?"

"Wait, you guys. I've fixed a nice supper. If you want go, go after supper. Ike, your dad brought home the full paycheck today."

They are all looking at the Jerry in a strange way. They have not seen this type of reaction of the Jerry nor an interest in the language. However, speech and understanding will be easier by learning the language and not having to go to the interpretation of the words in the Jerry brain.

"Well, that's a change. I will take him for you, Mom. I'll take him after supper."

The odor of the preparation of the sustenance—the food—is effortlessly apparent to the Jerry. He is quite anxious to eat the food that the Helen has put on the table. His body appeared again to need the energy despite its generous fat proportions. They all sit at the table. The four other members of the group watch the Jerry throughout the eating period. They sense a difference in the inhabited, the Jerry. Unlike the first host, the difference detected does not seem to pose a threat to the existence of the Jerry. There is a sense of fear of the Jerry, which emanates from the others. This feeling of fear is borne by molecules coming from the others and floating in the air. The air molecules are easily detected by the nose and interpreted by the brain. Learning more about the biped race is necessary, and the dictionary could be the source of some of that information.

The library is a cuboidal structure. It is placed between the roadways called Vernon and Blanchard. It is located in a place with many vehicles called a shopping center. The Ike points to the door allowing entrance to the structure. The door is made from the material extracted from the trees and has many configurations upon it. The Jerry can interpret the forms into meanings. He uses the neuronal configurations in the upper outer brain substance. The method used to interpret the figures appears somewhat difficult for the Jerry. It is a slow process but could easily be improved with minor alterations in the brain's circuitry.

"Okay, here we are. We can ask the librarian if there is a paper dictionary or if there is one on the computer you can look at. Miss Librarian, do you have some sorta dictionary? My Dad wants to look up something."

The person that Ike is addressing is a woman of mid-age, it seems. Her hair is a bright yellow color, but the skin is much darker than the Jerry's. She comes forward.

"Well, you could just look it up online."

"No, I wish to look up all the words in the language without using the machine, the computer you called it."

"You want to look up the entire English language?"

"For fuck's sake, Dad! Look up gnu and let's go!"

"Young man, watch your language! Sir, we probably have an old dictionary here somewhere. You cannot remove it from the library. We have a couple of hours until closing, but I will get it for you to read to your heart's content until we close."

She moves away to get the dictionary and is watched by the Jerry. It also appears her hair color is artificial and is done for attractiveness or for effect.

"You gonna read the dictionary! Ya gotta be kidding! We have two hours before closing, and we don't have any way to take it home. Just look up the fuckin' word!"

"I'm going to read it, and two hours should be sufficient if I understand the time correctly. Ike, you go to the Helen home. I will be able to find my way back."

"Man, ya've always been strange, but now you're losing ground, no shit. Well, maybe I'll hang around for a while 'cause I think you will give up pretty soon, and there should be something here for me to read."

The dictionary is very large and thick. It has a musty odor and the cover may have been organic material. The Jerry takes some effort to lift it.

It was difficult to incorporate at first, but with grooving of the circuitry, it becomes quite effortless for the Jerry to incorporate the words held within the dictionary The information is excellent. It gives us and the Jerry considerably more knowledge than we held previously. The subject of grammar was also addressed somewhat in the forward of the book, which will allow easier communication.

When the Ike returned, we had completed approximately three-quarters of the dictionary.

"It's closing time. So, what's a gnu, or maybe you didn't get past the alphabet."

"It's actually any of several African antelopes of the genus Connochaetes, having an ox-like head, curved horns and a long tail. It is also called a wildebeest."

"No shit. You actually looked it up and memorized it? You are strange, but it's better than the normal you. Let's go; the place is closing."

"Yes, what is in the incredible array of other volumes present in this edifice?"

"They are books, Pa. Some tell about real stuff, and some are just stories. Jesus! Are you from outer space? How much of the dictionary did you get through?"

"I read up to but not including the letter U, page 1534. At some other time, I would enjoy completing the book. I also perused a small section on grammar."

"Did you get hit on the head again or somethin'? Mom said that the shrink in court said you are a paranoid personality disorder. But they didn't say that you had any special talent or that you was some type of robot weirdo. What's going on?"

It is distressingly obvious that the consumed knowledge was inappropriate to the character of the Jerry. The new knowledge and skill must be divulged carefully.

"It is not, or it's not something that is of great concern, but I do seem to have acquired some new abilities. I believe these abilities are generally helpful and will be useful to us all. I'll explain anon. Let us depart for home in the large floating machine and greet your mother, again."

"Yeh, let's depart and anon again with Mom. Brother, you have flipped your lid."

"You do not have a brother, but two sisters, if I'm not mistaken."

"Yeh, yeh, let's just go home okay. We gotta get outta here before I do somethin' crazier than you."

CHAPTER 6

Exploration

Merge with and control Jerry again.

"Helen, I picked up this old book about the Middle East. Why was the Middle East such a problem area? How did it happen that an incendiary device destroyed countries and distributed radiation over the entire region? This country, Israel, appears to have been one of the pivotal areas. Why would there be so much emotion? What were the issues which led to the destruction of an entire region and the poisoning of an even greater area? What was that country, Israel? Does that country still exist? Why are the passions of so many directed to that area? Where are we now? Are we close to that area of the world? Is it now dangerous to visit? Who are the people, and where are they now?"

"Jerry, what's happenin' to you? We're in the land of Chicago, of course! And why do you keep calling me Helen? It's my first name, but I've used Bette, my second name, for years, and you've never called me Helen. And where are you? Ya haven't gotten pissed in two weeks. Ya got a raise at the factory. I don't even understand what you're saying half the time. You got religion or something?"

"We . . . as I am aware, are of the Christian Catholic religion, but I have not actively practiced this faith, nor did my family. I follow some of the directions prescribed by the writings, but until recently, I have not read the actual scripture or thought about its interpretation. Therefore, I do not think one could call me religious or belonging to a formed religion. I am best described as a heathen. However, somewhere in your background, there appears to be a relationship with the Jews."

"Jesus Christ! I ask ya a normal question and you give some great big spiel. What is it? What's happened to you? Why are you telling me about Jews in my family? Hell, I'm not even sure of the story myself?

Do you like me less than before? Do you wish me to call you Bette again?"

"I am happy to call you whatever pleases you most."

"I think I like Helen, Jer. I love you, and even if you are really peculiar, it feels good not ta be arguing all the time. It's even causing a change, a good change in the kids. Ike thinks ya gotta be some type of genius, and he thinks ya must have got a hit on the head. He says he heard of stuff like that happening. Did you get hit on the head?"

"I believe I have had blows to the head in the past, although I do not remember one recently."

"Maybe a miracle or somethin' like that, but me and the kids like how you are kinder these days. We don't want you to change back. Don't get hit on the head again if you can help it."

"I will try to avoid that. Tell me about the people of that area of the world, the Middle East. When I mention the name Jews, there is a surge within me, as if they have taken some sort of advantage of me, but I cannot find the actual memory of that occurrence anywhere within my memory. Is there an instance of that happening? Why, then, do I feel such emotion about this issue? What can you tell me about them so that I have an explanation of my feelings? Are they threatening our group, our tribe?"

"Well, they say that the Jews own most of the businesses in Chicago and ya sort of feel that they're takin our money and our American right, and they're not really American, although America is all broken up now. At least that's what you used to say. Why are you suddenly so interested in the Jews anyhow?"

"I have some things I must do. I have awakened again and have something I must accomplish. I am learning human history, and it is statistically very likely that the awakening might have to do with the Jewish people and the devastation of the entire area of the Middle East. There is a mission, and I will be involved in that task. What were the circumstances that led nations to be angry at the nation of Israel?"

"What mission? What are you talking about? You sound like a robot, although less than before. Well, whatever has happened, it's a whole lot better than before. So, I'll tell ya what I know.

The Helen appears to be somewhat agitated but clearly feels empathy toward the Jerry, because of his character change.

"The way I understand it is that the Jews used to be there, like in Israel, in the Bible, and then they left or were thrown out, maybe by the Crusades, but I ain't sure. I think some of them were always there or in some of the Arab countries. Anyway, like after WWII, they had no place to go, and they had almost been wiped out. Their old land was Israel, so they wanted to go back there. You know it's holy for them and all that. So, the UN decided to give them back some of the land. I think the Brits had kinda given them some rights before. So, they took some of the lands from the Arabs, or from England, or the Turkeys; I'm not sure who owned it. It kept being owned by other people. Anyhow, then there was all this fighting and wars, and the Jews got some more land, and the

Arabs wanted all that land back, although some of the other Arab countries were not so sure. And the Arabs are Muslims, which is another religion. But there are a couple of types of Muslims, or maybe more, and they fight among themselves. Then there are the Turkey people. I always think that's such a funny name. Like, could you ever think of being called the chickens or the cows or something like that? Sorry 'bout that. Anyhow, there was this group called the PLO."

"PLO, is that a country? I have not read about that."

"It stands for Philistines or something like that. Anyhow, they made some type of deal, and the Jews gave back part of the land on the West Bank so there would be peace. Y' know that was a sorta deal, that no more trouble with wars or anything like that should happen again. But, anyhow, they like some more trouble 'cause some of the Arabs in the West Bank wanted to go back inside Israel 'cause the Arabs were worse off than the Jews. But the Jews didn't want them back in the land. I don't know why. Anyhow, the PLO or I guess now the government of Phillastine or another group called Hamas or something, were saying the Jews are causing the trouble now because their own people are poorer and the Jews should share some of the money 'cause they took their land away for so long like without paying any rent or something. And there were other groups fighting and killing, so many of them, and a bunch or terrorist groups. Shite, and another one or two. So, there was a lot of trouble and it kept boiling. Now there were some other Arab nations, and some of them had been working on the big one. You know, the weapon that is sorta nuclear, but the radiation is not contained, like the new ones. The new ones are made so that you could drop it and just kill all the people in a country without the neighbors being affected. Actually, they were not able to do it, but they were able to buy it. So anyway, they wanted to do it cause of hate or something, and they were going to do it. But then the Israel people found out when they were trying to deliver it and boomeranged it somehow 'cause they couldn't destroy it. Nobody believed those guys would be stupid enough to try something like that. Nobody could believe that it could happen. People aren't animals, everyone said. But then some famous thinker said that people hadn't yet figured out they were not still living in small tribes and gotten over the hatred of the other tribes. Anyhow, they boomeranged it back at them and warned them. But the Arabs didn't make it right somehow, and the reaction kept going, and most of the area was destroyed, although they managed to neutralize a lot of it. A whole bunch of people were killed, and the Jews mostly dispersed everywhere in the world, but Israel is still there, although the other countries are in a mess. Do ya understand?"

"No, I'm not sure that I do. Where can I read about all this Helen, Bette?"

The Helen feels more affection for the Jerry as she puts her hand on his.

"You are weird. Here, Jer, read the Bible; that's a start. That'll tell you the beginning of them, and then the story seems to keep repeating. Then you can go to the library and watch all the reports in the news services about what happened."

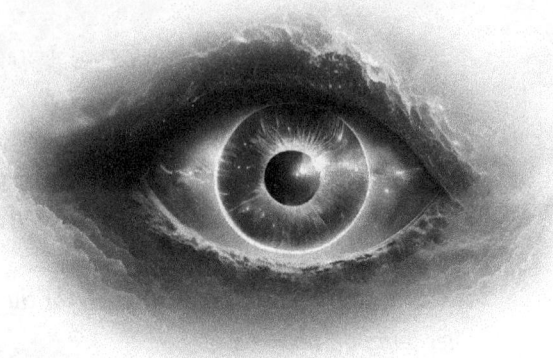

CHAPTER 7

The Bible

Merge.

"Helen Bette, I've completed the Bible, both of them, but I do not seem to have an appreciation for the trouble today with the Jews. Yet somehow, I do feel it is connected with that group or what is depicted in the stories."

"You read the whole Bible in a week, both the old and new? You got to be puttin' me on."

"The length of time was actually only a few hours, but I have been driven to listen to net news, and I have accessed the computer in the library and perused some of the many books and articles on genetics and the development of your species."

"Your species? What do you mean by that, Jerry?"

"Oh, I was just reading about our species, you know, homo sapiens. People here divide humans up by what they call race and sometimes religion. The Jews are people who are sometimes set aside, and yet, they do not seem to have enough characteristics in common to make them an actual race. In fact, DNA analysis of all the so-called races in the world does not show many differences, although there are slight differences in the number of ancient hominids mixed in the genes of the so-called races. Some groups are tribal or larger than tribal but bound by a subtype of religion. And then again, there are the groups arranged in countries. Most of the groups keep their identity by living in the same geographic territory for long periods of time. This allowed them, the French or the Irish, to develop similar language, culture, and broad perspectives on life. The tribalism and disappearance of some of the characteristics of the tribe seem to have caused war and ripped your nations apart. I'm not quite sure how the Judeans have managed to survive without territory for the centuries."

The conversation is taking place as Jerry is helping cut up vegetables for a salad for dinner in the room they call the kitchen.

"There ya go agin', Jer, with those weird words. Sometimes you seem almost normal usin' normal words and things, but not that old anger, and then other times just weird! Ya talking to God or Christ or what? You are talking like one of those prophets or somethin'. You got religion; I knew it! Has God spoken His words to you?"

"God, the one Supreme Being who appears to have evolved from the mountain thunder deity of the Levites. It is difficult to say whether Abraham or, more correctly, Uvruchum talked to the one God or simply his God above all other gods.

"There ain't many gods, Jer. Just one God."

"I think Sodom and Gomorrah had many gods. People made idols that represented gods; even David had idols in his house. Then, of course, there were the gods of the Greeks, the Romans, the North American deities, and many others. Furthermore, from what I can gather, people often pray to the same God to help them defeat other tribes who are asking for help from what seems to be the same Almighty being, God. And God is expected to favor one group over another if they worship or believe in just the right way. It's in the Bible, and there are punishments, horrible ones, for not listening to the word. But the words differ somewhat depending on the belief system adopted by the tribe. Also, the God in the Bible seems to evolve from a God of a mountain to an omnipresent God who rules or oversees all the living things in the world. And then he seems to have a son, which adds more complexity. And then, of course, there are all the other gods of antiquity and the ones of many of the tribes existent today. So which God do you mean, then? Perhaps that will help me understand your statement."

Helen drops the knife she was using to cut vegetables and shakes her head.

"God! There's only one God, for God's sake."

"Perhaps you are correct, Helen. Perhaps just one who has been understood differently by all the different groups. There, of course, is always the possibility of none. That mankind simply needs to control the people by the creation of an all-powerful overseer.

"Jer, there's another strange thing I've been meaning to ask you about. I know there's something different or wrong. Now, I don't mind that you think you're a prophet or something. The prophets was good men. You've been real nice to the kids, and Ike is starting to really look up to you like he should to a dad. And Jer, when you're nice to me the way you are, it makes making out kinda special. I really enjoy it."

"I sense what you enjoy, and I also have pleasurable reactions doing it, making love. I remember another experience similar, but different, where a female demanded the intrusion. It, too, was pleasurable and . . ."

"I don't want to hear about your past experiences, Jer. Especially because now things have never been so wonderful between us. I dunno what happened to you, but it's wonderful. There's another thing, though, that I don't understand. Why did you take out that large insurance policy? I saw the papers on the table. Also, you seem to have a problem with automatic doors at the shopping center. What is that?"

"Well, the insurance. A Mr. Elfenbaum came to speak to some of us in the factory. One of the guys, my fellow workers refer to themselves as guys, whispered that Elfenbaum was a Jew. I already mentioned to you my fascination with this particular group, and since I have not met any person who acknowledged that they were from that group of people, I wanted to speak to Elfenbaum. It is unlikely from reading your history that any particular person has an understanding or cultural memory as to what forces actually formed them or what brought about those forces. Nonetheless, I did wish to speak to Jason Elfenbaum about it. I believe that this is a piece of a puzzle that I need to understand. It is associated with my reason for being here. He agreed readily to meet with me, but as I suspected, speaking to him did not enlarge my understanding. He did not wish to discuss religions, but the things he had to say about security for you and the children seemed to make sense in view of my recent past experiences."

"What past experiences?"

"I have experienced the unanticipated cessation of brain wave activity, death, quite unexpectedly, in previous hosts."

"Hosts? Ya mean at a party when you got in a fight and was decked? I remember you being unconscious and you waking and not knowing where you were. I know your old pals. You're not going to do somethin' bad again, are you? Are you going to get into a fight, or the controllers get you or somethin' stupid like that, are you, Jer?"

"No, I have no resolve to participate in an illegal act or something which might result in my death. I don't wish to deceive you. I am not talking about me, as you know me. I am speaking of previous lives. I have experienced a life where the lifeform was stung to death and another shot. Where is San Francisco?"

They are now sitting on the couch in the living room, and Helen clearly feels very close to the Jerry. She moves closer.

"Jer, you're scaring me again. You mean you believe in reincarnation and stuff. Remembering old lives? And San Francisco? Jer, what are you talking about? I'm getting really getting scared. Why do you want to know about San Francisco? Please explain these things to me, but don't change back Jer, don't change back to what you were before. You won't, will you, Jer?"

"I assure you that there are now many permanent changes in Jer, in me, and I will never be the same again. In a way, I do believe in reincarnation, at least for me, and not in the usual way that people have written about it. I have never encountered a soul or spirit world to which they refer. But I have experienced other lives, but I would rather not discuss that at this time. On another occasion, I will explain more of this to you. It is difficult to understand, and perhaps it is better for you not to know. I will deliberate on this matter and elaborate on this issue subsequently. As for San Francisco, I am interested in the fact that they have had those earth slides in the place called Los Angeles and an earthquake a number of years ago in San Francisco at the time of an important baseball game. I know nothing of baseball, but the cities and the disasters remind me of a similar disaster in the Bible. I do sense that those cities have something to do with me, but I am not certain as to the reason that they may be important."

"Jer, when you answer me, I still don't get most of what you're talking about. It sounds okay, just as long as everything remains like this for a while. Maybe at least explain this to me, Jer. Why don't electric doors to supermarkets and stuff open for you? They used to."

"It is better that you ignore my ramblings. These are random thought processes and not relevant to everyday life. Your question is appropriate for daily existence; why do the doors not open at my approach? An elementary explanation is required. When one passes through the light beam, it activates an electromagnetic circuit which activates an electric motor. The motor activates, then opens the door. Once an individual walks through the beam, the other circuit is again completed, and the door closes. I don't break the beam because of the energy I release. It is of no consequence. How would I journey to San Francisco and Los Angeles, Helen?"

"I still don't know what you are talking about, Jer. And what's this interest in those places anyhow? They're in the United States and just down the west coast. It would take too many credits to air there and money and a lot of time to use something like the shooter to get there."

"What would be the most inexpensive way to travel there? I would not want to use up the currency which seems so necessary for you and the children."

"There is no inexpensive way to get there! If we had a car or an emats, maybe you could take your holidays and go. But we don't and can't afford either yet! Maybe, maybe if you keep working the way you are, we could afford one, and then you could go. But we need you here, Jer. You were never here in the past and never there for us. Ike was always in trouble, but he is now starting to look up to you. He is just coming around, and he needs you so much. We all need you, Jer. I used to be a wild one, too, but since the kids, I felt a responsibility. You never settled, but now you have. It's what I always hoped and even prayed for. I thought it would never come."

"I register pleasure at your delight. I am not certain what path I may take, but events and people change with influences upon them. Hence, things cannot be the same once they are acted upon. Whatever the experiences of the future, you, Ike, the girls, will never be the same."

Ike had entered the room and heard the conversation about San Francisco. He interrupts Helen and Jerry and is excited.

"Dad, I know this place where you can buy old parts of motors and stuff and build it yourself. I think you can rent the tools and everything. Did you read in any of those books or videostructs how to build a car? That would be seprific!"

"It should not be a severe obstacle. I will go to the library and read the segments *apropos* to building a car or Emats this afternoon. Tomorrow, we can go and investigate the place you mentioned and decide whether it would be possible to build a vehicle. Would you enjoy that, Ike?"

"That would be frosted sperific!"

There appears to be joy on the face of Ike that the Jerry has seldom seen.

"I do not understand everything you have stated, Ike, but this is something that may help me, and it seems that it will bring you pleasure. Few situations benefit all participants, but this task does appear to be for two. A task for two, alliteration; I believe I am developing a sense of humor."

"Jer, I don't understand what's goin' on. I'll go along with ya, 'cause I think I trust ya now, but I don't know what's happening. I know Ike will enjoy learnin' stuff like building a car or an Emats, that's good enough for me. It's just like I hoped it would be, spending time with our son. I'm sure he's your son, Jer, no matter what. I just know it."

Both the Helen and the Jerry turn to look at Ike and then at each other. There are pleasurable sensations in the Jerry's brain.

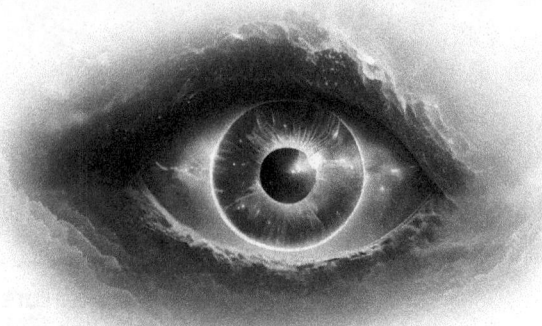

CHAPTER 8

The Wrecking Yard

The garage is situated on a large lot with portions of the transportation devices known as automobiles lying in layers in several areas that were numbered, presumably as a method of retrieval. Although the internal combustion engine was still in use, most cars are either battery-powered or are the conveyance known as an "EMATS" (electromagnetic transport system).

The Emats, although quite different in the mechanism used to power the driveshaft of the vehicle, was often referred to by the same name as the older vehicles, which burned a combustible material, the internal combustion engine vehicle. Both mechanisms of conveyance were called cars. The name apparently derived from a horse-drawn cart known previously as a carriage. The Emats was the emerging popular transportation vehicles when shooters were not used. Shooters were private rail vehicles, which travelled, most often, between cities, although shooter rails also ran through cities on any electrical track available.

I think we, I, may anticipate a problem with the Emats. The device uses a reversible energy field to drive the flywheel, which may be interfered with by our energy field. Shielding would have to be arranged so that the Emats will function normally.

Ike is running back and forth to the various stations in the wrecking yard. He appears to be quite invigorated by the prospect of assembling a particular kind of Emats he had previously selected from a compuview. He directs the compucrane to select several body and interior parts we had hitherto listed. These were selected from the compuview menu of parts. The compucrane will deposit the parts in the reconstruction area. The recast bays contain the tools and instructions necessary to reintegrate the components together to build the Emats. The motor, the driving force of the Emats, was simple in its design. Many of the vehicles and motorized conveyances noted on the streets had similar contrivances, all used to convey people without the use of their own power. The city shooter-like appliance, used to travel to the factory on a daily basis, was built on a different principle.

The compucrane should be studied carefully. It is not malfunctioning despite my proximity, although not shielded.

How much shielding the Emats would require to operate without interference would have to be carefully calculated. Even a small amount of interference could lead to . . .

"Ike, move away quickly! The electromagnetic hoist is malfunctioning."

Move the Jer quickly, as it's necessary to throw Ike immediately out of the path of the falling, must save Ike PAIN!!

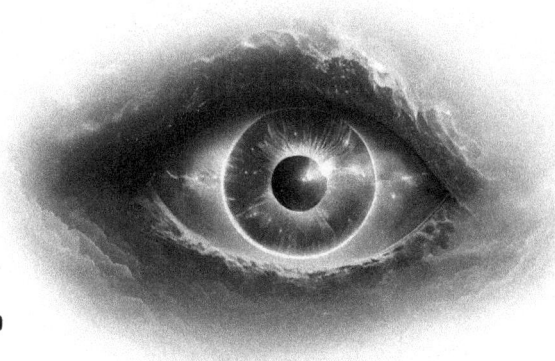

CHAPTER 9

Abbie Baby

"Abbie, baby, are you awake yet? Come on. Hey, are you okay? You look kind of strange."

"Where are we at present?"

"Abbie, what's wrong with you? You look like you've seen a ghost."

Old Abe stopping my streaming for a moment. I have not looked at my younger self for so long. Handsome dude, I may say. Average height but slightly curly black hair, sometimes falling over one eye, and neatly trimmed beard. Handsome devil, if I do say myself.

"I've got to build a car, an Emats, for Ike. Also, we—I—will drive it to reach San Francisco and Los Angeles."

"Honey, you must have had a dream. We are in L.A. You made it a long time ago."

Settle down. It was difficult getting here, but we made it. Who is this Ike that you're dreaming of, anyhow? I don't recall anyone of that name on our travels?"

The brain wave patterns are different than in Jerry, and yet similarly constructed. This is a new host! Something has happened to Jerry. Jerry must have terminated, died. A blow from a falling object from the compucrane evidently caused the brain death. What happened to Ike? Was there time to thrust him out of danger? This will have to be explored. I am happy that the insurance policy exists for them. They are important, and I will miss Helen and Ike especially. Our focus on Los Angeles and San Francisco has brought us here.

This host is also a two-brained organism but with a higher-developed left half. There appears to be a greater mathematical ability as well as an aptitude to dream, hypothesize, and plan. The rest of the body is built essentially equivalent to that of the Jerry but with less bulk in the middle of the body. The DNA is essentially identical, so this being is a human as the group defines itself. The human being may not stand as tall as Jerry. Its muscles are less bulky, but it appears to be a better-honed individual, both in its mental aspects and physical character. This individual is also a male.

All the people wear artificial covering or clothing because they have no fur like the forest creature. They have developed hairlessness. One wonders, however, what the advantage would have been to drive this change. It is difficult to imagine. Perhaps a greater attractiveness for females may have been the selective feature.

The brain is rather fascinating. There is a balanced interconnection to the right brain, the predominantly emotional part. The rage of the Jerry is not there. It may not be mandatory to control this organism, as the Jerry had to be controlled. This brain has rage and anger, which can be accessed, but there is greater modulation. Greater control of the emotions is possible for this human being than the previous one.

There is the awareness to sound vibrations reaching the brain, coming from the female human in close proximity to the new host.

They are in an enclosure consisting of many rooms, one of which is a kitchen, as it has some similarities to the apartment of the previous host. They are not in a building like the Jerry host, but the dwelling place seems stand-alone. Looking out through the glass, greenery, flowers, and other similar dwellings can be seen.

Submerge and observe.

"Abbie, what's wrong with you? You look strange. Are you having one of those guilt attacks?"

"No. Something strange seems to be happening. I feel like I've been dreaming, but about things I've never experienced. Guilt? Look, honey, I'm sorry. I will always feel guilty about what we had to do to get here. But if you hadn't played up to the 'king,' we wouldn't have gotten the passage card. We would never have escaped before the nuclear holocaust. If we had not gotten to the no-longer united states of America, this whole family would have been in trouble. You know the devastation. I had to help my brother's family as well as my nephew, Lloyd, his wife and girls, everyone! God, I don't know why all these emotions are playing out right now! I feel like crying. It's like I've lost my best friend, several friends!"

"I don't want to talk about your crazy relatives. Lloyd's kids are wild ones, and I don't approve of their brand of morality. Lloyd is a worthless no good, despite the way you've set him up. They're just carrying on the way they've always done. Anyway, enough of them. I've got you, baby, and I've never been so happy and so free."

"I'm happy, too, and excited about our future. I know we are now on the right road, in the right place, at the right time, Seri. Two of us, leaving just before the nuclear catastrophe in the Middle East. Leaving Israel, our journey to Ontario, and now in the country of California. It's been quite a trek. We've left desolation behind and had losses on the way, but I feel we are at a new beginning."

"So, if that's the case, why were you so deep in thought just now?"

"I had the strangest feeling—like someone was carrying out a conversation about me in my head."

The woman is shaking her head and sitting down on the couch.

"God speaking to you again, Abbie!"

"That was just for the balconies. No, just a little hallucination or something. I seem to have my head crowded with stuff. I seem to have words floating through my head as if I had memorized the English language! This is really quite strange! Would you get that ancient paper dictionary on the shelf in the den?"

"Here, what do you want it for? That's an antique. Tell me the word you want to look up. I bet I know the meaning, or we can look it up online."

"I don't want to learn a particular word. I have this funny compulsion to read the damn dictionary from the letter U onward. I don't know what's going on. It's the strangest feeling. I wasn't even thinking about it, but when I saw the dictionary, it was as if I had some unfinished work to do."

"Do you feel okay, Abbie? You looked a little strange a few minutes ago. Do you want some coffee or something?"

"I don't feel quite normal. I don't feel sick. I almost feel energized. Do you know what a gnu is?"

"Yeh, I think it's some kind of African antelope or something like that. May I be so bold to ask why you are asking?"

"I dunno. Actually, it's any of several African antelopes of the genus Connochaetes, having an ox-like head, curved horns and a long tail. It is also called a wildebeest."

"Abbie, are you for real? What are you talking about? Is this a joke? Are you practicing one of your magician's tricks?"

"No, it's strange, Seri; this is no trick. I know that's the correct definition. As a matter of fact, I can see all the words in the dictionary, like turning the pages of a book in my head. It's like I'm scrolling through a computer screen. But I can't see past the letter U. Strange, huh?"

"Abbie! What's going on? I've never seen you act like this. It seems to have happened so suddenly. Did you have some type of stroke or something? It made you like a savant. That's it; you just had a fit. You were very still for a few minutes and then you started acting strangely. You definitely had a stroke or a seizure. Don't move. I'll call the doctor!"

"Sarah, Seri, take it easy. Don't panic. I feel okay. You don't have to call anyone, except . . ."

"Except what? I'm calling a doctor."

"I'm okay, Seri. Calm down. I don't feel sick at all. Don't get worried so quickly. Worries are a thing of the past. Now look, I am very well and more settled than I normally am. I'm even quite calm. Calmer than normal. It's just that I have this feeling, a funny sensation, that someone else is here with me, kinda inside my mind. It's not uncomfortable. Weird, really, but not uncomfortable. It's okay. Seri, I know it's okay."

"I want to have Harold Newberg look at you. Phone for an appointment!"

"It's Sunday, and I'm sure he doesn't have office hours on Sunday. He's too well-established. He can afford the day off."

"Abraham, let's be calm. You're having a hallucination or something. You're imagining someone is talking to you. I am talking to you, but no one else is, Abbie. Now stop reading that dictionary, put it down, and call Harold. He'll see you at home; he's a friend, and he'll do it for us. Let's go over there. He'll see us!

"Sarah, first of all, I don't need Newberg. He's a neurologist. If something has happened, it's more that I've finally flipped. So, if I'm crazy, I need a psychiatrist. Secondly, although I feel slightly strange physically, I feel perfectly well. I am quite aware of reality. I do not hear any voices other than yours. It's not like that at all. I don't feel ill, and I don't hear, see, or smell anything unusual, and I am imagining nothing. I guess that's not quite true. My sense of smell seems to be heightened."

"Abbie, you haven't called me Sarah in years and what do you mean you're not having hallucinations? For God's sake, you're reading a dictionary!"

"I do want to read it. I can't quite explain that or the feeling I have, but it's not like hearing voices. It's kind of a feeling of a presence. And I seem to be able to absorb all these words while only partially concentrating. Perhaps I have become a savant, or maybe I've just tapped into a sleeping portion of the brain. But I feel so well, so I just cannot be sick in any way!"

"Oh, Abbie, what's happening? You're out of touch. Things are going well and becoming stable after all the turbulence and travel. We're no longer wandering everywhere from place to place. God, please, don't let something happen, not now!

"Hey, Sarah, Seri, settle down. Everything's okay. Nothing is wrong with me. I feel wonderful! You know, we should get a dog. I feel a kinship with dogs."

The Abbie is sitting with Seri and puts his arm around her shoulders, pressing his lips to her cheek.

"Okay, you feel normal. It's just that you have a visitor who is talking to you about a dictionary. That seems to be a normal thing to me, not! You are going to come with me right now, and we're going to the emergency room!"

"I've never felt better, and because of that, my wife wants to take me to the emergency room. Look, Seri, if it makes you feel better, I'll go, but we've got that coverage for 'Dial a Doc' through the business.

They have 24-hour coverage and they're scratching for a living. Some of them are even driving taxis. They can drive right over, and we can go on a cab ride while he's doing the diagnosis."

"I thought you said these were just young kids out of medical school, but you hired them to cover the people in the wool shop."

"Listen, I protect my flock. Docs are so hungry nowadays. This group gets their pick of the crop. These guys had a good business plan, and what's more important, they're dedicated. I went over their transcripts from medical school and they're excellent. I think they provide an excellent service. Furthermore, we pay upfront, but we can get a rebate at the end of the year if the company doesn't use the service. So why shouldn't I call them? Now, do I really sound crazy?"

"With you, it's always difficult to tell crazy normal from crazy. It is just that now you have stepped over the line. Right now, you don't sound much different than your normal insanity, but call anyhow."

"Look, I'll call, and I'll make the appointment. We'll go out for a little lunch, drop into the doctors and get my head examined. They'll commit me for a few hours, put me in an immobilizer, and then we'll go to a sensiround at the new theatre. Now does that sound like a reasonable plan for an insane fellow?"

"Okay, Abbie. I am worried, and I really wouldn't drag you there if I didn't have some concerns. You must admit your behavior is a little odd. I'll get my sweater."

"Take your time, Seri. I'll call and make an appointment, and then I'll just finish the dictionary."

This inhabited, this Abraham, can sense our presence. A full merge is not necessary with this inhabited. At the present time, great control does not need to be exerted. The character and function of this host's brain are more compatible than with any of the others. Observation can be accomplished without control of this host. It will be possible to direct this person with no dulling of the personality of this Abraham. There will be duties to perform to fulfill the mission. This Abbie, this person, must be better protected than the previous hosts!

Resources must also be used to help the family of the Jerry. Time is passing, and the Issue is approaching and could be devastating.

The dictionary that the Seri gave the Abbie is also thick, like the one the Jerry had. It is heavy but does not smell musty. There is a faint scent of but difficult to place from our experience on this planet. The cover is hard and related to the paper inside.

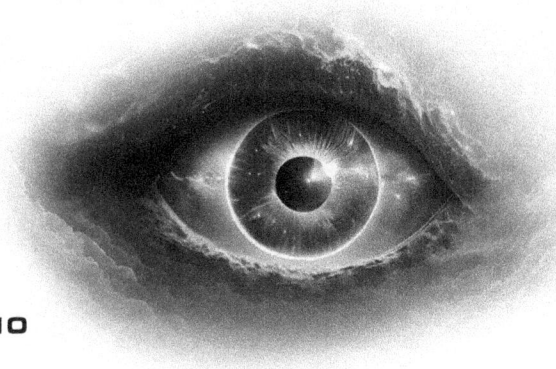

CHAPTER 10

Clinic

The Abbie and the Seri are now in a building with many apartments. This one was labelled Dr Sim, Caldwell, and Ramm, Physicians. They enter a room with a desk at the front and several rooms behind labelled exam rooms. Abbie is called into one of the exam rooms and the doctor enters.

"Take a deep breath through an open mouth while I move this ultrasound equipment, Mr. Benterah."

"Whatever happened to those old stethoscopes? Why are you imaging my chest? I don't feel at all dyspneic, Dr. Sim. My wife's worrying about my mind, not my chest. I think you should train that thing on my head. Can those sound waves penetrate a very thick skull?"

"We'll look at your head presently. Sometimes, if you have something that bothers your chest, it can decrease your oxygen supply enough to make you confused."

"I'm not hypoxic, for God's sake. I'm not cyanotic. I have no fever, chest pain, never smoked anything, don't even try to get the stuff through my skin. Doc, you're more confused than me."

"Have you had any medical training Mr. Benterah?"

"Nope, I just know some of the words. I picked those up when perusing the dictionary. I only knew the dictionary to the letter U, except I actually never really read it at all, except for after U, which I have now completed."

The doctor looks at the Jerry with concern while sitting back in his chair,

"That does not make sense, Mr.Benterah. You must have read a portion of it. Not a whole lot of people read dictionaries, Mr. Benterah. Do you keep rereading the sections up to U for any particular reason? And what did you mean that you actually did not do it?"

"I have since read the dictionary from U to Z, and only once. I seem to remember reading the other part at another time, but I know I have never done that. And yet, I can see the whole thing. All the words. It's not easy to incorporate the words into everyday language, you know. That's another skill. Something else has to get connected for that to happen. Interesting, that. I can give any definition, but I really have to think about it to pull a word into common usage, convention, form, practice, habit, custom, fashion, formality, manner, mores, observance, routine, tradition, use, way, wont. Those latter words happen to be synonyms of common usage. It's amazing how much conversational language. I didn't know even though English is almost my first language."

"Very impressive. Yes, your wife told me you had been reading the dictionary. How long did it take you to get through U to Zee? It must have been a mammoth task. You must have been very dedicated. Did the compulsion to read the dictionary interrupt your sleeping habits? Were you able to eat throughout the time it took you to finish the task?"

"I did it from the time I woke up from a nap this afternoon. I didn't really do it all in that time. I already knew A to T, so I only had to finish U to Z. I had had a good night's sleep, and I had breakfast. Maybe it took me an hour, but probably less. I intend to take my wife to lunch, so I don't think my compulsion, as you labelled it, had a significant effect on my lifestyle. So, Doc, I don't think I really have a compulsion."

The Doctor Sim is looking at the Abbie with concern, and the brow is furrowed.

"Tell me, Mr. Benterah. Don't you find that type of behavior just a little strange? The average person doesn't page through dictionaries or even use them anymore since you can look up words online. And yet you attempt to memorize all the words and believe you can do it. Do you really believe, in your heart of hearts, that absolutely nothing is out of the ordinary here?"

"I did not fail to note that I had acquired an ability that I did not possess before, well, today. My memory has become photographic. I do not have to study the words; just look at the page. Somehow, I feel comfortable with that. Intellectually, I know that my behavior is just a tad more eccentric than is usual for me. However, I don't feel unbalanced. Something is very orthodox with me. What is perplexing, however, is the first part of the dictionary. You see, I know it. I remember reading it, and yet I recognize that I never did. That is a little bothersome, and I guess I should get excited about it, but I feel quite calm. It is almost as if someone else read it and transferred the information to me."

"Where are you right now, Mr. Benterah?"

"Well, if I interpret your question in concrete terms, I'm right here beside you, Doc, and if you don't know where you are and have to ask, then we should trade places. However, if this a test to tell you whether I am oriented to time, place, and person, then it's the twenty-eighth day, Nisan, 5983."

"You really believe we are in the year 5983!"

"Actually, it's funny the way that came out. We are in that year by the Hebraic calendar. But I don't know how I know the exact date because I don't really use that calendar. There are a lot of things I seem to know that I should not. By the way, it is Sunday, the 18th day of April, 2570."

"So, you do recognize that your responses are abnormal. You do have some insight into that. Now, what other abnormal thoughts do you have?"

"Well, I experience the dictionary. I don't have the words at my fingertips, but I have them available as if I were reading a compuscan. I'm not sure exactly how I acquired that ability, but it's there. I see it, feel it, can touch it. I seem to see it all, page by page, and I can just kind of look up the word I'm thinking of. It's as if I am looking at the compuscan, but I just have to visualize a word or a page, and it's there, right in front of my eye, except in my head."

"Have you felt particularly less powerful recently? Has something or someone made you feel small? Do you know what I'm getting at?"

We can tell by the Abbie's thoughts that he is not happy with where this is going with the doctor. He does not completely trust this man, but he has decided to carry on telling him how he feels.

"I do feel there is something else present within my mind, but it doesn't seem to bother me. I neither feel impotent nor potent. I feel pretty klutzy at the moment. But you asked me before if I feel normal. So, I will answer you in this way. No, I feel normal, although people will tell you my normality is eccentric."

"So, you feel normal, but you cannot really be sure, and you can memorize dictionaries and have a fund of knowledge you shouldn't have, and yet, this does not make you feel powerful."

"Powerful or omnipotent, mighty, or supreme. Nope. Can't say that I do, strike 2. I recognize that this is just a little unusual, but I'm not feeling anything weird, and I'm not upset. Something tells me that everything is okay. These abilities are part of the new me. I have been a little bit reborn, but not in a religious way. There will be some type of rational explanation for all this, and when it comes, I know I will be satisfied, even if others may not be. I trust that everything will work out. I'm not going to fight this thing. It seems natural, and I'm going to go with it, live extemporaneously if you know what I mean."

"All right, Mr. Benterah, let's call your wife in and because I think you are suffering from delusions. You need a referral to someone skilled in these things. Medication may be needed, but I'll let someone else decide that. Do you have anyone in mind that you would feel comfortable seeing? Oh, hello, Mrs. Benterah. Come right in."

The Seri enters the room and looks concerned.

"Is he okay, Dr. Sim?"

"Just to review this thing for you, I believe your husband has a fixed delusion, and therefore, I think he should see a neuropsychiatrist. He may need medication or just a minor bit of surgery to divert the circuit that keeps reverberating in his brain. I'm not sure about the cause, but I'm not as skilled in those areas as a neuropsychiatrist would be."

"Look, you two! There is absolutely, positively, nothing wrong with me. I'm not going to see any neuro-response manipulator or anyone else. I did this for you, Sarah, but honey, enough is enough. Now, let's go to eat."

"Mrs. Benterah, your husband believes he can memorize all the words in the English language, and that faculty just developed this afternoon! He also initially told me we were some time thousands of years in the future."

"Horse manure! Hmm, why would I say that? Anyway, the year is 2570. The other year I quoted was not in the future but today by the Hebraic calendar. It kind of stuck in my head because I was looking at the Hebrew calendar not very long ago in the library, although it wasn't me at the time. At least I don't think it was me, but I have his memories, or are they my memories?"

"Mrs. Benterah, I strongly advise another opinion with haste. I even might suggest commitment, except

I do not think he is dangerous to himself or anyone else at the moment. Having said that, I think he should see someone right away to confirm that."

"Another opinion is that you're full of bullshit rather than manure. Do you want a third opinion? If I were you, I would wear heavy underwear to keep your brains from freezing. Do you want a fourth opinion? Never mind, there is no mind to never. Sarah let's go. I've been insulted enough for one day!

The Abbie is agitated and angry with the doctor. He is not going to physically lash out at the doctor as the Jerry would have. He jumps up, bangs his hand on the desk, and grabs the Seri's hand.

"Abbie, what's going on? All the doctor wants is for you to see someone else, a specialist."

"I think I've been manipulated enough today. It's time for some fun and frolic before getting back into the salt mines tomorrow. Let's leave now, and I want something more than lettuce for lunch. By the way, doctor, you'd better get your doors fixed. They don't open automatically anymore. I was able to obtain my morning exercise just trying to pull the Goddam thing open."

The doctor shakes his head as the Abbie and the Seri leave the room. He appears concerned.

"Goodbye, Mr. Benterah, Mrs. Benterah. I hope you'll take my advice. I am trying to help you. I believe

I am giving you useful advice. I strongly advise you take it."

"Sometimes advice is useless even if it's not given away freely. Come to think of it; we've been on our plastic timer since I got in here. Let's get out of here before they drain it dry."

"But Abbie, I am really concerned about the way you are acting. You're just not normal! I don't know what to do, and you're scaring me."

"You should have concern, my love, but not because of any abnormality in my brain. My circuits are as balanced as they have ever been. The concern is for the world. I have an awareness, an intimate knowledge, that we, the world, are destined for a change. The change may be something quite beneficial, even glorious, or some type of catastrophe. It is up to us, to us all."

"Abraham Benterah, what are you talking about? This is supposed to calm me down. What is this about circuits, the world, oh, Abbee!"

"I'm talking about the world, about destiny, about events that are larger than this room, this planet, this world. I'm talking about a balance, an order, where now an imbalance of anger and hostility reigns. We need to add a dose of serenity and calm. We need to restore a sense of purpose. We need to dialogue about a greater plan, a true vision for the world that all living things will share."

"And most importantly we need lunch! You know, Seri, I am talking a little crazy. All this chatter and prophecy has really piqued my appetite. I feel quite ravenous. Can we go now, please? I really want to do lunch."

"You sound like a raving lunatic!"

"Why? Just because I want a little lunch? Honestly, Seri, I know I sound crazy, and I feel just a little looney but also as wonderful as I've felt for years. Quite suddenly, I feel my life has real purpose. You must believe in me. You must be beside me, you and the whole family, our son, Helen, Ian, Lloyd, his girls, even his wife. We are all in this together."

"Our son! We don't have a son and you know I can't get pregnant! I am 52 and perimenopausal! And who are these other people you're raving about? Who are Helen and Ian??"

"You are pregnant, Sarah, and it will be a son. I felt it when I touched you. I was able to extend my energy into you somehow, and another being was there, Sarah, another developing being!"

The Abbie and the Seri are walking to the parking area as the Abbie is talking. She stops and stamps her foot, shaking her hand.

"Abbie, you're frightening me! You will see someone, just like the doctor said. You know I can't get pregnant. We've tried in vitro fertilization and egg transplants, and I've prayed and bargained with God. Abbie, how could you say such a thing? How could you be so cruel? You never were a cruel man."

"Are you my pregnant wife? Search your feelings, Sarah; search within yourself. You will discover the truth of the statement. I know I sound a touch maniacal, but tell me, have you felt anything like that at all? Be honest."

"I did have the weirdest dream last night. God blessed be He. I dreamed a messenger came from Him and told me that I was to bear a child and that he would be destined for something great and . . . what am I doing? Your craziness is infectious. Abbie, I'm so scared and worried about you. Please, please, please, stop all this and go get some help."

"I am not crazy, Sarah, and I don't think that's the type of help I need. Yes, I have been acting strangely, but there are things that I know, and I just have to say them. Please don't get religious on me. What is happening will have an explanation. I know everything is going to be all right."

"Abbie, you need big-time help."

"Seri, I don't, and I do not need to see anyone, but boy, do I need lunch."

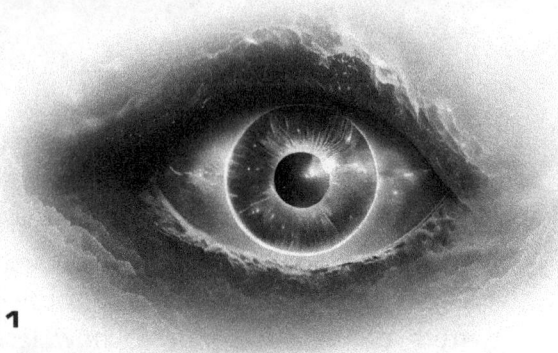

CHAPTER 11

The Analyst

The Abbie has entered another office in a building similar to the previous one, which held the doctor. There is only one name on the door, Dr. W. Naivir, Psychiatrist.

On entering, the waiting rooms have only four comfortable-looking chairs, and no one is at the desk in the room.

The doctor comes out of an office and motions the Abbie to come into the room.

"What brings you here to see me, Mr. Benterah?"

"Thank you for seeing me so quickly. I've come because my wife is going nuts. In some marriages, if one partner is going nuts, the other sees a psychiatrist. There must be some sense in all that. But I need to help her, so I am seeing you."

"So, you do not need to see me, but your wife does? Is that what I am hearing, Mr. Benterah? May I call you Abraham or Abe?"

"You may call me Abe, and truly my wife is very upset. I need to do this to help settle her down."

"Okay. Let's focus on you for the moment. I am interested in some of the symptoms you started to display that were outlined by your doctor."

"I think you should know that there is nothing wrong with me, except I seem to have suddenly developed some unusual abilities."

"So, there is nothing troubling you?"

"No."

"Then why are you here?"

"As I stated at the outset, my wife is very worried about me, and I wished to ease her mind; no, I wanted her to stop worrying. Sometimes my sentence structure gets so dammed stilted that I have to fight with myself to make it normal."

"Abe, it sounds like your wife should have come for the consultation since she is the one that apparently has the problem. I must be interviewing the wrong person. There is absolutely nothing bothering you, I take it, even though you mention a little problem with your sentence structure."

"Well, I do have a feeling of another presence, as well as the sentences, and there is a feeling of knowing people and places I've never met or seen. And, oh yes, there was the compulsion to read an ancient dictionary from U onward, and I guess there is the little problem with certain types of automatic doors."

Dr. Naivir is a tall woman with what the humans might call a pretty face. Her hair is thick and black and white. She appears to be the same age as the Seri.

"What do you mean another presence? Could we explore that a bit?"

"I want you to know, madam, that there is nothing wrong with my mind despite what I have just defined. It has been improved. It is more precise, and the capacity to memorize and rapidly absorb knowledge is quite useful.

I have a concern, however, if we were to admit to these abilities, that it would be interpreted as a mental aberration and that surgery or drugs may be used. These are dangerous methods and are not at all necessary."

"I'm an analyst, Mr. Benterah, and I do not prescribe drugs. Drugs do work, sometimes, but even in the light of modern knowledge about neurotransmitters and in what area of the brain many symptom complexes arise, most drugs still are not specific enough. It continues to remind me of the old analogy of using a shotgun to kill a fly. Sometimes I enjoy using ancient expressions; they seem to be more believable than modern ones. What I mean to say is that there is still room for talking about a problem and linking it to your past in order that you make your own neurotransmitter change just by thinking about it. You, yourself, can make a very specific change. Although the drugs have some specificity, basically then, the medication just blasts at various tracts, so we hope that with the right stimulation on the patient's part, there is a resetting of the behavior patterns."

The doctor stops and looks at the Abbie to see if he is taking the discussion in. She pauses and then continues to talk.

"Analysts, on the other hand, still feel that by going over the ground carefully and in-depth, we can be much more specific in understanding the personality and give that understanding to the individual. Then change is more a matter of choice for the individual, and as I mentioned before, it can be more exacting.

Now, I hope that detailed explanation has eased your mind in terms of what we may or may not do."

"Well, that is a relief that you don't want to give me any mind-altering drugs."

"According to your doctor, your wife is worried that you are breaking down, or perhaps even developing multiple personalities, which is a term, by the way, that we have pretty much discarded. I don't believe in the concept, at any rate. However, I did detect a change in the pattern of your speech. Perhaps that's what you meant by being stilted in the speech pattern. At one point, you referred to 'if we would admit to these abilities.' Do you believe someone else is speaking for you, Abe? Am I speaking to Mr. Abraham Benterah, or are you an alternate personality?"

"I am pleased in your views of medication and surgery. I detect that you are trying to be helpful.

I am concerned about this place, this area of the country. It is to us a certainty that the cities of Los Angeles and San Francisco will be destroyed or rendered chaotic. This may not be an immutable fact, however, but to be safe, I advise leaving the city in the near future."

"Are you Mr. Abraham Benterah, or is this someone else I'm speaking to?"

"I'm Abraham Benterah, of course. By the way, do you have a dog?"

"Good, now, when did you develop this feeling that L.A. and San Francisco will be destroyed?"

"There is a problem Dr. Naivir, in that you are concerned about my mental status so that any utterance I make is counterbalanced against a background of mental disequilibrium. But just presume, rather than being erratic, my mental aberrations are rather trivial. In that case, what I say may actually have validity. The only way to disentangle this situation, Dr. Naivir, is to test my proficiency against my assertions. The claims should be effortless enough to probe. Do you wish to test my expressed capabilities with something in this office?"

"I'd rather hear why you think those two cities should be destroyed. Is it something to do with good and evil?"

"Whether I feel the cities should be destroyed is of no consequence. I do not know anything about the cities or the presence of good and evil. It is just that I feel strongly that there is a lack of harmony here, and the cities will be rendered dark in some way unless something can be changed. People have to be identified to save the cities, or people have to leave."

"You will not be responsible for this destruction?"

"I will endeavor to identify individuals who, because of their personal characteristics or their positions, the cities will be preserved or will not go dark. If that cannot be accomplished, then I will undertake to at least evacuate as many good people as possible from certain chaos."

"If you wanted to, could you destroy the cities yourself? Do you have the power?"

"No, Dr. Naivir. That is a preposterous statement."

"A little while ago, you said 'we.' What did you mean by that?"

"I must have been using it in the grandiose sense."

"I also feel that your speech patterns seem more stilted, at least some of the time. What's happening to you at those times? Do you feel there is someone else emerging?"

Submerge.

"Well, Doc, I know you feel that I'm definitely a fruitcake, nutty that is. But, you see, a person is not paranoid if there are really people chasing you, and you're not psychotic if you really have acquired knowledge in an admittedly strange way.

Sometimes when I think about the questions asked, I feel that someone or something in my mind is kind of prompting me, and at those times, I know that I talk unnaturally."

"So, there is another presence. Do you know who or what this presence is? This other presence is the reason that you used the term 'we'?"

"I suppose there might be another presence. I don't feel that some little green man or a giant rabbit is talking to me, if that's what you mean. It is just a feeling that there is something different. Sometimes I almost seem to be observing myself talking without control over what I am saying. Sometimes I don't feel that I have total control of my thought processes."

"Does this other presence have a name?"

"Not that I am aware of. I am not sure there is another presence. It is certainly not a person in that sense. It's just that I feel something else is in my mind, in my body. It has also endowed me with something else, a sense of smell, a clarity of vision, and some of the unique qualities that I've mentioned. There are times I view myself as speaking. I am talking but not quite in control of the words. So, I don't feel that I'm completely in control. But I always seem to know what's going on. The question of L.A. and San Fran just popped into my head, and then I had a certainty of its truth. Maybe I am just a little bit crazy."

"You don't seem to be bothered by the fact that you're not completely in control of all your speech. Is it that you do not feel that it's very unusual that you have the power to see the future, to change it, to have an extra sense of smell and reading ability?"

"Strange it is. Psychotic, it is not. I don't have visions or anything like that. It seems I just have a special knowledge, kinda shadowy, of things to be. And I really do have special senses. These enhanced senses are real, not imagined. Now, if one can genuinely have a shadowy view of the future, and that future seems catastrophic, shouldn't one try to change it?"

"I would agree, but how do you know for sure? Do you really believe that the future is laid out and is not random? What is your experience with this, Abraham? Does this not have a ring of unreality about it?"

"I have no experience, but I have reverberant knowledge. Perhaps the One and Only, Blessed be He, does not play dice with the world."

"Do you think that you're a messenger of God, Abraham?"

"That quote was from old Albert E, not God. I don't exactly know what's going on, but I certainly don't feel serene like I'm some holy messenger. It's a little strange, I guess. Hey, I don't know what to think, Doc. I just know that I seem to know a lot. I have some extra senses. I know I should just keep quiet about all this, and something inside me is telling me to shut up, that this is dangerous talk. What am I doing?"

"Abraham, are you back with me? Your speech in the last few minutes has lost the stilted quality. Perhaps this other self of yours has gone. Is the other self the messenger? Perhaps we can explore that, the messenger as really another aspect of yourself."

"I just feel extra energy and knowledge or something. I also don't turn this on and off like a switch. As I've tried to explain, this is just a feeling. There is not another personality, no messenger, just something else up there. I don't feel that I'm psychotic. I know what I'm saying sounds somewhat bizarre, but I also know it's what I feel. I should stop talking about all this."

"Abraham, have you ever contemplated suicide? Are you going to be destroyed in these cities?"

"Doc, I'm not suicidal, and as far as I'm concerned, I don't want to die in any catastrophe. I just feel that a major calamity is coming, and somehow, I must do something to prevent it. I also feel that, not unlike many others, our civilization has gone in the wrong direction. I feel in some way, I can bring things more on track and possibly avert a tragedy. Having said that, I don't know exactly what I must do and how I can make any difference. I don't know what's coming down or who I should report to. I know it sounds like I feel I have been speaking to God or some deity, but I haven't heard any voices or seen some burning bush or anything like that. If I feel that whatever I do, the disaster will occur, then I'll evacuate my family and whoever else I can convince and head for the hills, maybe to another promised land, to start civilization over again."

"Our time is up for today, Abraham. Do you wish to see me again? I can give you a time in two days and then perhaps work you into a regular schedule if you wish. Perhaps we can work out why you think you have to be a savior. Perhaps there is something in your past which has to be recalled. We'll talk about it all. Meanwhile, you won't go running off somewhere, will you?"

"Well, Doc, I'd like to see you again because these things do seem to be becoming clearer for me, and that's helpful. I don't think I have any messiah complex, but I'm willing to think about it. There are just two more quick things, if you don't mind, before I leave."

"Perhaps we could discuss this next time."

"Well, I was wondering about the payment for this session?"

"There is a standard fee I informed your wife about at the time of the appointment. It is coming automatically off your credit accounts. What is the other question?"

"Would you google the definition of any word that comes into your head, and I will give you the exact definition."

"Our time is up, Abraham."

"Won't you humor me?"

"Perhaps next time."

"Okay, but 'next' is on page 964 in the dictionary I read, and 'time' is on 1485. That was before the U dictionary."

"Goodbye, Abraham."

"Goodbye, Doc, and goodbye, Mrs. Calabash, wherever you are. I'm off to see the wizard, and I'll follow the yellow brick road. Gee, I hope the good witch of the north, or was it the east, is looking over me. Bye, bye, begum, beepum, beepum, beepum, gebee, gebee, gebee, that's all, folks. Crazy, no?"

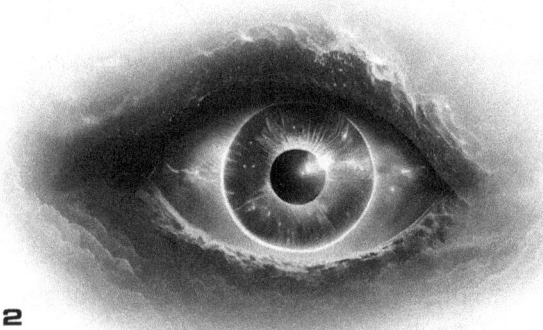

CHAPTER 12

A Look At The Past And The Future?

The Seri is clasping her hands together and waiting for the Abbie at the doorway of the house.

She is pacing.

"Abbie, how did it go with Dr. Naivir? Did you get along with her? Did it help? Are you feeling normal?"

"I guess so. I feel she is trying to help, but I got a little angry at the end of the session, so I made a little scene as I left the office."

"Oh, why, Abbie, why? Can't you let your pride down and let someone in there to help you? There's something wrong with you now and you know it. So, stop with the being smart. Let her help you! I need you strong and clear-eyed!"

"She refused to take the Pepsi challenge. Sorry, honey, that's an old joke. Not very funny. They used to challenge people to some test to distinguish one carbonated beverage from another. Anyhow, I'll be seeing her in a couple of days and apologize. I will try to let her help, but whatever is different about me, and I know something is, it's not wrong, nor is it mixing my head up. Well, maybe about a few things. Anyhow, I will try tomorrow; tomorrow is only a day away. Today I have to go see Lloyd in San Francisco."

"Abbie, I don't think you know what lowering your guard is like, even with me. You're a very secret person, really. I would be surprised, maybe even jealous if you should tell this doctor all about the real Abraham, the one who doesn't always make with the wisecracks. So, why do you have to see that no god nephew of yours anyway? He's nothing but trouble, and you have enough head trouble now without getting that no god involved in our lives again. You have helped him enough!"

"I think you mean no good, not no god."

"I think that wasn't such a slip."

"Look, he is my nephew. I have felt responsible for him since my brother died. I agree that his wife is a little crazy, and half his kids are no goods, running around and doing I don't know what. But they are family, and I must try to help them help themselves. Furthermore, I will have to try to convince him to leave San Francisco with his family and avoid the disaster. He is friendly with a lot of people there;

perhaps he can help me ferret out the good people of that berg and bring them out with him."

"You don't mean to tell me you want a whole bunch of people to leave the city, do you? They will definitely feel you are nuts!"

"You never know, if there are enough people that I can convince, together we may be able to muster the type of help capable of averting whatever will happen. That's why I need the good men and women. It's to marshal together enough brain power to identify the cause and correct whatever will happen. I don't know exactly what to do, but I feel I must do something."

"It may be easier than you think to get him to move, although I don't know what help he can be to anyone. While you were out, Norman, Lloyd's friend, called. Lloyd's in trouble again with one of the kingpins in San Fran. Who knows with that man what he's gotten himself into? He's probably desperate again for money. Abbie, Lloyd's probably got some mean, ruthless, probably horrible friends. If they're after him, you could get caught in the middle. Hear me, Abbie. I do not want, do not wish you to go."

"I'll be all right, Sarah. I have always been able to take care of myself somehow. We've been in some very tough spots before, and we survived. I must be blessed. I also have a duty toward Lloyd and his family. I cannot stand by and let him perish in some holocaust, which I feel with certainty will come. I must try to help him; he's kin. We must take a voyage, and it is important that we are all together. It will be a new beginning."

"Voyage? What voyage? You want to move again? Where do you want to go? You're starting to sound strange again, Abraham. Oh my god, what are we to do? Where do you want to go, Abbie? We should all go to San Francisco?

"No, we must take all our goods, family, friends, our flocks and wend our way to Winnipeg."

The Seri is pacing back and forth, waving her arms. She is upset with the Abbie.

"Wend our way to Winnipeg! Where's Winnipeg? What's Winnipeg? What flocks? Oh, no, no, no! Abbie, get a grip, for God's sake. Wake up; you've got to get control of your mind, grasp reality!"

"Winnipeg is in the province of Manitoba and in the country of Wescan. It is an area that has lost its developmental force since the ancient type of rail travel became obsolete a couple of centuries or so ago. The land of Manitoba is filled with lakes, rivers and streams, which are relatively unpolluted because of the sparse population. It has fields of grain, wildlife and a population which has deserted it. It will be the new land of plenty, of milk and honey."

The Abbie is trying to calm the Seriqwqwe; he holds up his hand palm outward.

"I know, I know, it even sounds mystical to me when I hear and see myself making these pronouncements. It's true, Seri, it's right. Look at this place; look at how we live. Afraid to go out without protection, deals with the power brokers, the newsmakers, whoever. Our life is not free but ruled by immoral forces. There are no positions, no right things, wrong things, only shades of grey. Shades of grey are okay and, in fact, are very important in order to develop a free and accepting society where everyone is welcome regardless of religion, color of skin, or gender, etc. However, you do need laws that will guide the society. Unless there is some strong guidance, not based on religious rules, but an overall, overarching law, your society eventually will fall apart. It can draw no line. This can be done with religion, but that is dangerous, as we well know.

The Abbie is excited. He holds Seri by her shoulders and talks earnestly. He is on the correct path.

"We either need to change society or go to where we can rebuild society, new rules, or at least a return to the old, to the laws of right and wrong, good and evil and a little in between. I can't believe I am saying this, but you know, Seri, I believe it! I cannot see how we do this right now, but I know we can somehow work it out."

"First of all, Abraham, what's with this thing Wescan? Aren't we talking about Canada? That sounds like a land of ice and snow. Your milk and honey will freeze! We are doing well here, wonderful, after such a bad start. When we came across after the Destruction, we had so many trials. Abbie, I even had to pretend to be your sister so your parents could bring us in like a family. Even then, as a young girl, I had a crush on you. I didn't want to be your sister. But I had to pretend. We all had to pretend so much. I don't want to think of it now. You dealt with the powers that were, you made them respect you, and you managed to forge a path for all of us. After years in this country, we've straightened out our lives, and we've made it. Life's not perfect, but we know the rules now, and we can deal with all the problems. Why start again? We have just begun to live here. I am happy. Abbie, I love you, and always have, since I was a girl. I looked up to you, admired you. But this is too much. I am not going anywhere. No, we're not going anywhere until we get to the bottom of your mental imbalance! You have to see the psychiatrist again!"

"Sarah, all those troubles are in the past. The future holds nothing like it. It promises a new beginning for us and ours. Perhaps it will be a new beginning for everyone. What we did in the past, we had to do. We had to immigrate to this country after the Destruction. My parents had to pull every trick they could think of, to get us all in. You know, there were funny immigration laws at that time because of the fears that the severe radiation sickness that many of the immigrants had might be contagious or that they would use up health care. Also, there was the concern about bringing in malcontents, terrorists, which again raised its head. We had to prove we would not be any problem to the Health Care system, although there really wasn't much of a system left. My parents didn't have the proper papers for you, so you became my dead sister, Sarah. May she rest in peace. I know I had to play some charades with you as we moved across the country, but we had to, and we did. We proved we were not a burden on society and had to pay them off with the only currency they would accept. I'm so sorry and guilty, but we did what we had to do. The future is nothing like that. This will be our land, our country, and we will make the laws. The laws will be just but real. We must build a society not built on technicalities. We have a chance to build a new society. We must take that chance."

"I know, I know. You told me. I believed God made us do it. I agreed. I've put all those old memories in the past. We did make it, and it was with both our efforts. We did our part. I was not a passive member, Abbie. I wanted you and the new country and knew what to do. I am, or at least was, happy. But now

God is talking to you again? I love you, my husband, but I'm scared. I came with you here, a joint effort, a goal we worked on together. I want to be with you anywhere. But to move again after all we have been through. And to Winnipeg? Cold, deserted, nothing up there but ice and snow. Why go there when we are doing just fine here? It's crazy, Abbie. Crazzie!"

"What's so crazy, to want to move, to a new land, a better place, a new start for all of us? This is crazy?"

"No, it's not crazy. But you're not moving just because you want a new place. Suddenly you have this . . . this messiah complex. You think something is going to happen here and that you can prevent the catastrophe, or if you can't, stop something from happening. You have to save people from whatever it is you imagine is going to take place. Uvruhum, you are not acting normally. You think you can memorize books. You tell me I'm pregnant at my age, at 52 and menopausal, and after all the radiation we've been through, and you even tell me the sex of the child. Then you want me to pick up everything we've built and wend to someplace called Winnipeg! Other than that, the last day or so has been quite reasonably uneventful, and I really do not know why I should be upset at all!"

"That's what made me fall in love with you in the first place, Sarah—when you were my sister. You have that stability and sense of humor no matter what."

Cosmic Eyes

"Abraham! Stop calling me your sister! I was just sort of adopted; you know that! Please, Abbie, you're making me crazy! I'm not being funny. I'm desperate and don't know where to turn. You suddenly want to move, to make a better life for us and develop a better civilization. Where did this come from? You are not telling me the whole truth. You are doing something for some other reason, and you're not telling me. Why? What is happening?"

"Sarah, I don't know what to say. After the pain we experienced in the beginning, I don't want to cause you any more anguish. But something is different about me, and it's difficult to explain. There are only two explanations as I see it."

"Tell me, Abraham, I'm listening. What are the possibilities?"

"Well, the first one is that I'm cuckoo in the coco, something that you strongly suspect. I have to admit that my actions may have given some credence to that hypothesis. The other possibility, however, is that I'm not on the mental skids. Now, if you acknowledge the possibility that my mental apparatus has not been turned to the off position, then it opens up some interesting options. These include the prospect that, somehow or other, I have gained the ability to see into the future in some limited fashion. The same somehow or other has left me with the ability to memorize all sorts of things. The somehow or other has turned some mental gears so that I suddenly remember or know things that I can't know. It's like reincarnation or something. I don't believe in reincarnation, but I have a memory that I have been things, seen things, of which I should have no memory. I have the sensation and knowledge of what the wet forest floor feels like under my feet. I won't describe the feet. You'll think I am talking werewolf. I have the sensation of hunting and not with a rifle. I know intimately what the inside of an insect hive is like, probably a beehive. I have lived with another family, in another life, and I have died in all those lives, only to be reborn into another. There is more, but I don't want to make your eyes widen any more than they are now. Maybe it would be better if I had a knocked noodle."

"Are you telling me that you really are psychotic?"

The Seri stands with her arms outstretched and then holds her head.

"No, I said there were two alternatives. The second one that you kind of ignored is that I've been telling the truth or that what I am feeling is really happening to me. I don't know how it's happened, but it has. Perhaps there are ancient memories that can be turned on in the mind. Perhaps the environment or certain experiences can be imprinted on the genes, and then the genes can transmit memories, just like patterned or instinctual responses. I don't know, but I do know that I am experiencing this, but I don't feel any more disconnected from reality than I ordinarily am."

"Look, Abbie, even if what you say is possible, you've been talking about seeing into the future. Now, you have been the one to tell me that prescience is impossible. You can't see into the future; no one can. So, I can't believe the second possibility, either. Abbie, please try to come back down and speak to me. Whatever is eating at you, we can discuss and work out. I know you've been under stress."

"No, you're right. I can't exactly see into the future, as in sensiround, but I have more of a feeling of mathematical probabilities. So, it's not the real future, just the most likely future. The future can evolve differently, but that won't happen unless someone changes the input. Then the formula remains the same, but the outcome is different because the input is different. Understand?"

The Seri puts her hands on her hips.

"Oivey, oivey, oivey, Abbie, come on, come up for air. You are really going off the rails. I can help if you let me in on what's happening."

"We can play a word game again. Pick a word, any word, and look it up on Google or whatever."

"Not the gnu game again."

"It's a concrete way I can show that I do know what I'm saying. Can you explain that ability by my having suddenly become psychotic? Nothing else explains my sudden ability. Now, give me a word."

"I'll make you one of your little deals. If I look up a word for you and play your game, will you then settle down and play mine? Just talk to me, and maybe we can get to the root of what is bothering you so much, Abbie."

"If you give me a fair shake at this, I'll try to help you understand me as much as I understand me."

"Okay, you've got your deal. Here, I am going to scan here; let's see. No, wait a minute. I am going to open a page of that old dictionary you were reading.

The Seri moves to the shelf and brings down the dictionary.

"Here we go. What does the word 'pleonasm' mean?"

"Pleonasm, page 1106, the use of more words than are necessary to express an idea, redundancy. Should I go on?"

"Sanguicolous."

"Living in the blood as a parasite, page 1266."

"Abbie, that is impressive! How do you do that? Is this some type of trick? It really is weird, Abbie."

"I don't know how I do it. I have developed an incredible memory. I don't have to try and remember; I just do. That's the problem, and it does not make me crazy. In addition, all the predictions I make, I think are true. I have a certainty, at least in a mathematical way. Everything I've said I believe is true. That includes the prophecy regarding the birth of our son. We can prove if that vision has substance by going to our neighborhood shopping center and checking it out on one of those ultrasound machines. Not only will it tell you that you are pregnant, but if the position is correct, the computer will tell you the sex. But if you believe me, then the next question is how do I know, and where did I get the ability? Here's the real scary part and why I agreed to see the analyst. It's also why I've got to return to Dr. Naivir. I have got to understand more about the working of the human mind. So, you don't have to force me to go back to the analyst, I want to return to see her and try to understand my inner mind and perhaps bounce some thoughts off her."

"So, talk a little more slowly, Abbie. Explain this to me. What is it that you are feeling? What is this scary part? You think you have ability that you didn't know about, and that scares you? So what are you saying, Abe! Where do you imagine you acquired the ability?"

"I'm saying that there is something different about me. I feel there is something up here, riding with me in my head. It's like I can talk to my mind and answer myself, with answers that I shouldn't know. And yet I don't feel in a panic about it. I can imagine in my mind seeing the ground from the air in an entirely different way than I've ever seen it. It's like I'm looking out of someone else's eyes or maybe something else's. I don't actually see anything; it's just that I have an extremely clear memory of the landscape from above, with colors more vivid and different than I have ever seen. I can feel into people when I touch them. I seem to be able to follow up the nerve tracts, enter the brain and follow the activity, and just know what they're thinking and feeling. I even feel I can change those thoughts in others by reaching in along those tracts and adjusting neurotransmitters. I even have an amazing sense of smell and can interpret those scents accurately. This is no trick, and it's not like looking into some crystal ball. I've had some type of brain implant when I was asleep and have taken on the memories of the implants, and there are several of them, not just one. I don't feel I have different personalities, but I know I have known other people and things. Perhaps it would be better if I was crazy."

"So, what are you saying, Abraham? Are you saying that you're possessed? Have you been abducted by aliens and returned?

Maybe you have multiple personality disorder? I think they don't believe in multi-personalities anymore. It went the way of the dodo, whatever a dodo is. So what? What is this thing that has given you these amazing abilities? Are you becoming ultra-religious again? Is God revealing himself to you as you thought he had in the past? Are you on that kick again? So, is He actually speaking to you and guiding your actions? Is that what you believe?"

The Abbie leans back on the couch in their living room and holds his head. He is trying to understand us.

"You know, I was young at the time and couldn't quite understand myself, so I thought a higher power must be speaking to me. It was a delusion. I am not saying that now. I'm saying that something else is with me, or someone slipped me some new neurotransmitter stuff which is very long-acting or something. If this is some type of strange new drug, it sure is believable, and I'm still in contact with the real world. No matter what I feel, I have to go along with these thoughts, at least part of the way. I want to try to save San Francisco and L.A. and I feel it's within our power to do so. It's what I said before. I think they will be destroyed or at least disappear in some way. But if I can change something, somehow it will change the whole equation, and I may save millions of people, good people, bad people, but most who are somewhere in between. These folks are just moving along, doing their own thing and unaware of the fate that will befall them. I know there is no fairness in the world, but I have to give them the chance. That's one of the reasons I have to go see Lloyd. If we can't convince him and his family, then how can we convince anyone else?"

"Abbie, what do you mean 'we'? Are you talking about us? Or do you believe that God or an angel is with you? Is that the other person you are talking about? Are you afraid to admit to me that you're seeing visions again like before when you brought us here? Abbie, I think I know you after all these years, and very little that you do will really surprise me, although I have to admit that you've come pretty close recently. Listen, if He is speaking to you, we have to listen! Abraham, I can't forget that once before, you had this fantasy, and yet you convinced your parents to leave the land of Y'srael before the tragic Destruction to the area. You really led the way from Israel to America. It's hard not to believe in you with that type of track record. So, I do believe in you, Abraham, and will go with you where you want to go. But please be sure what you want to do. Then, if you're sure, meerchesam, we will wend our crazy way to Winnipeg.

"Sarah, my love, I don't know if this is the one and only or the creature from beyond, but something or someone is inside me, and yet I feel it's okay. Thank you so much for your support. It's very important and allows me to go on. And I've got to go on to San Fran. San Francisco is in major danger, and I must try to save the city. I don't know if I can, but I have to try. If I can't, then I must save Lloyd and his family. So, I'm off to San Francisco. Let's have them open those golden gates . . . here I come."

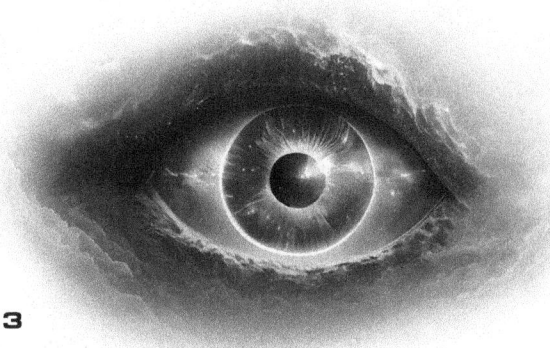

CHAPTER 13

San Francisco

The Abbie is in another apartment building. He walks up to a door and bangs with his fists on the door. He hears voices from inside. One he links to Lloyd in his brain, but the others are unknown. He is in the city of San Francisco. He is anxious.

"Okay, I'm coming, I'm coming. You don't have to keep knocking. Who the hell is it?"

"It's Abraham. May I come in, Lloyd?"

"Abie, uh, Uncle, look, I've got some company. Maybe you can come back later. These guys have been knockin' on my door for a long time. Give me a teleview in the morning."

"I believe now is of the utmost importance. It is imperative that I enter your dwelling place. God, what am I saying? Lloyd, cut out the evasiveness and lemme in now, you idiot."

"What! I told you, Uncle Ab . . . Abraham, I've got some important people here. Teleview me later."

With our help, Abbie is able to interfere with the electric circuitry and open the door.

Hey, how the fuck did you open that door!?"

"Damned if I know. I just was able to read the electrical signal and generate it somehow. How the hell did I do that? Anyway, oh, how do you do, gentlemen? I'm Abraham Benterah, Lloyd's uncle. Pleased to meet you."

There are two large men in the room with the Lloyd, who do not look happy. They have a facial expression that is probably described by the word 'scowl.' One of the men who looks like the leader is speaking.

"Boggs, help this gentleman to the door. We're not finished our business here tonight."

"Look, I'm sorry to interrupt Lloyd's business, but it is really important. If you gentlemen wish to listen, I will also explain how important this is to you as well. As a matter of fact, this is an important message for you, Lloyd, and for the people of this great city. You and your friends should leave this city because I have reason to believe it will be destroyed or at least disappear in some way, and I don't think anything can prevent this from happening."

"Uncle, what the hell are you talking about?"

"I know it's cuckoo nephew, but I feel calamity will happen, and I feel I can do something which might avert the oblivion. I don't know why. Sounds stupid, no? Anyhow, all the way down here, I was thinking of the Torah, believe it or not. And somehow, I do believe that if I can prove that, you know, like in Sodom and Gomorrah, if we can find a few good people, then the future I see will not happen. But what does it mean to be a good person or an evil person? Isn't goodness and badness just relative? Somebody does something, but there was some justification; 40 years ago, 80 years ago, his mother left him, he didn't know his father, he was high when it happened, or low, or there was an indiscretion, whatever. The behavior is understandable, perhaps even forgivable. Is there absolute good, is there evil, or just people and reactions, all stemming from our humanness? So, this allows a society with rules to operate as long as the action, the blow, stops short of my nose. But what is mine, and how far was my nose sticking out? Perhaps the nose met his fist rather than vice versa. No, it's very hard to keep straight. But I know we're back to the fundamental rules of tribalism, territory, bluff and intimidation. I know that I'm babbling out of control here, but what I think is important is to change people's perspectives on the rules that a civilized society should have."

"Uncle, people are too invested to change the rules now."

"Really? After an evolution that probably took us to the greatest experiments in human civilization, with some breakdown in tribal barriers, the old rules came back with a vengeance. We lost the ability to tell when the given freedoms went to freedom from any control. This absolute freedom may have been the seeds of our own destruction. How can we change all that? It's not going to be possible after what I've seen. We have to develop a society not based on a deity or cultural background but accepting of each other, with the commandments as a background or something simple like that. If that could be quickly developed, just like in the Torah, we could save the cities. But I don't think so. I do not know how it could possibly happen within a short period of time. I know I have verbal diarrhea here, but do you know what I'm talking about here, Lloyd?"

"I don't, Uncle."

"The drug kings dominate these two cities, and it's no longer helpful that drugs are legal. The strength of the drug companies and the helplessness of the people just make the society ripe for the pickings. They are now atop our cultural feudal system and have added to the depravity that heretofore had existed. We must, ooh, you are hurting my arm, Mr. Boggs! Please release me!"

The leader is getting angry.

"Push him out the door. We have business, and I don't wanna listen to any nutty talk. Now do it Boggs, now!"

"I must warn you, Mr. Boggs, that despite this pain you are inflicting on my arm, you must stop. God! There I go, with my brain taking over my mouth before I can think about it. I mean, how does that happen anyhow? Look, Boggs, I will cause you some injury. I will endeavor to make it non-permanent."

"Get him out!"

"You got it Steper, out you g . . . !"

The Abbie has learned to integrate and change the circuits. The Boggs falls to the floor.

Now the Lloyd is very worried. He puts his hands to his head and speaks loudly.

"What the fuck did you do to him, Abbie? Do you have a weapon? Is he dead?"

"No, I have just paralyzed the peripheral nerves distal to the T4 nerve roots. He can breathe, even talk, and will recover. I am not precisely certain of the number of minutes it will require for the recovery to be complete."

"I am Mr. Steper to you, Mr. Benterah. You're a dangerous man, although I would not have thought it. I don't know what you did to Boggs, but it isn't going to happen to me. Do you know what this is, Abraham?"

"I believe it is a revolver or a gun, Mr. Steper, a metallic tube from which missiles or projectiles may be forcibly expelled after the ignition of powder. There are more modern ways of directing rays to cause harm to living organisms, but they generally are large and not conducive to transporting on one's person. I can't seem to get out of the two-talk mode. Look, Mr. Steper, I just need a little time with my nephew, and then you can go ahead and carry out whatever business you have for him. I should tell you, however, that I will . . ."

"I don't have time for this shit, Abraham. I'll now demonstrate how this revolver works . . ."

"Uncle! Oh my God! Steper! You shot him!"

"Genius must run in your family, Lloyd. I just can't figure how you came to that brilliant conclusion. Don't touch him, Lloyd. You can look after that after we've settled our business."

"He'll die. Steper!"

"He's probably dead already. Now, as to the situation regarding the distribution of the pharmaceuticals we were discussing before we were interrupted. As I have mentioned, you will distribute them from your shop as per the agreement with your wife. Talk about tragedy, your uncle here has just suffered his, and you will get yours if you in any way, in any way, you understand, screw up! You have no choice in this matter, and you will do what I say, or you and your family will lie as low as your uncle is now."

The Lloyd looks at his uncle lying on the floor and back at Mr. Steper wide-eyed and open-mouthed.

Merge.

The missile passed through a portion of the lung, and the inferior vena cava, above the renal veins. It has not penetrated the thick-walled high-pressure vessel, the aorta, which leads the blood away from the heart. There is time as the heart still functions and the brain is being supplied with blood. The clotting mechanisms have been mobilized, but fibroblastic proliferation can be increased to seal the rent more rapidly. Growth factors are being deployed, but these can be augmented and the disrupted area repaired to make the clot more stable. Oxygenation is dropping as the affected lung has collapsed. First, control both the thrombosis and the thrombolysis in the area. Smooth the clot. The two openings in the lung parenchyma are now sealing off, aided by the growth factors and the proliferation of the acinar tissue. The lung must be re-expanded. The air in the pleural space surrounding the collapsed lung must be released. Create a small gap between the ribs by parting the parietal pleura, the intercostal muscles and the skin. This can be done enzymatically by locally activating those appropriate lytic varieties and dissolving the tissues. Create positive pressure in the deflated lung with a temporary ball valve. Expand the chest; the lung should inflate slightly, try to force the trapped air in the pleural space to the exterior. Now . . .

"Okay, okay, but Steper, let me give my uncle mouth-to-mouth or something. I've got to do something to try to save him!"

"You can try but it will not work, Lloyd. Boggs, you're with us again. Good! Lloyd, see if he is dead if you want. Boggs, if he is, throw Abraham's body into the Emats and come back and pick up Lloyd here."

The Lloyd moves to the Abbie and applies positive pressure by blowing into the mouth. It helps expand the lung past the ball valve. Air is released to the exterior, expanding the lung. Close the plural fissure to the exterior. Release the ball valve mucus plug. The lungs are both expanding satisfactorily. There is flow without leaks in the vena cava, and the heart may return to a regular rate. Oxygen carrying capacity of the blood appears almost as before, probably, at a functional level for the Abraham organism. Normal respiration restored. Vena cava normal with no obstructing clot. Blood pressure normal, healed."

"That's enough Lloyd. Leave the body alone. Boggs, pick him up and put it in the Emats. We've spent too long here and don't seem to be getting anywhere."

"Okay, you know, Steper, there is hardly any blood at all. Don't you think that is kinda weird? Hey, I . . ."

"Boggs, what the hell is wrong with you? Boggs, Boggs . . ."

"Abraham, you're alive, and Boggs seems to be frozen!"

"I am, Lloyd, Mr. Steper. Now that I am touching the revolver, I do not think you will be able to pull the trigger on the device. I believe it now should feel quite uncomfortable in your hand."

"Abraham, what's going on? How come you're not hurt? How did you do that to them? They're just standing there frozen!"

"I do have some physical defects, but they are mild and temporary. As for the Steper and Boggs individuals, they have been neutralized temporarily. It's just a matter of stimulating the correct nerve impulses and reprogramming the brain in the correct fashion.

Now, how the hell do I know that? What am I saying? I feel . . . I feel like I've been watching a sensiround! Lloyd, to put it mildly, I've become a real weird dude, or chap, or man, bloke, whatever! Anyhow, grab whatever you want, Lloyd, and let's go!"

"Abbie, what the hell is going on? How the hell did you do all that? You should be dead! They shot you!

And now suddenly, you are up walking and talking, but talking a little strangely."

Merge.

Exposure of these gifts has almost led to the death of this host and has resulted in considerable difficulty with this host and his wife. We must submerge subtly, and the powers must be hidden, at least to some extent. Perhaps lying will be the best path to follow. We will have to watch carefully. He grabs the Lloyd's arm and tries to get him to the door.

"Abbie, Abbie, are you okay? You're not moving. What is happening?

"I'm okay, Lloyd. I am sorry. I was distracted for a moment. Let us leave quickly."

"But Abbie, we have control of the situation now! With this power you seem to have and my know-how, we will be unstoppable. We can do what we want, and they won't be able to touch us. Honest, I've been mostly on the up and up in my business dealings. I've refused to do the dirty work they've asked me to do. They finally busted into my house and started to strong-arm me. You know my wife, Gloria. She wanted to go and make a deal with them, and I don't know what type of deal she made, but the next thing I knew, they were here demanding something or other. But listen, you know the situation. The San is just like a city-state now, within this great US of A, which is no longer really a country. Thank goodness for our ultimate freedom! Now, we can really make it big, Abbie! If you can control that power you've got, we can operate right on the up and up and be protected by scaring them. We'll be a haven in this town for those that want to feel safe and deal straight, and we can charge big time for that. We can make huge money. We just have to give the public some demonstrations about your power! The public won't have to worry about the likes of Steper and people like him. We can be pretty straight, get a little protection payment, and I won't have to worry about Gloria going off somewhere and making deals. It will be good for us and everyone. And we'll be rich!"

"I feel quite rich, Lloyd . . . rich in thought, feeling, and love in my life. If I have been given a gift, then we must use it for the common good and not to accumulate wealth. I think I am beginning to understand my powers and my gifts. Now that I am not manic and I am not experiencing hallucinations. This is real. If what's happening to me is inarguably real and not crazy, then my predictions about these cities may or, at least, could be prophetic. Therefore, I have to warn the city of its imminent peril and the menace threatening Los Angeles. If the calamity to the cities cannot be averted, then we all must depart, defect, flee, high tail it out of here. We will wend our way to Winnipeg across some of the big skies in the western states to the cold, bleak prairies beyond.

The weather will change again, and we will find good land to till, raise our sheep, and clean our mutton, as we take it on the lamb. Phew, I think I'm getting my perspective back again. God, my side hurts."

The Abbie holds his side where the missile passed through and takes a big breath.

"Uh, Abraham, I think we have a miscommunication here. Wa-hat are you talking about? Do you realize the opportunity within our grasp? We are talking unlimited credit here! What destruction is going to happen? What the hell is Winnipeg?"

"Look, Lloyd, love that alliteration. Something has happened to me, and you have just witnessed some of the changes. In addition to the magical tricks, I have a prescient hunch that something will go wildly amiss in these two cities. There could be a lot of death here. I don't know why, perhaps, because the human experiment has gone wrong. Perhaps it is a natural disaster that cannot be changed, but I sense that is wrong. So, what do we have to do? Do we have to change the society, our neighbors, all the men and women, and kids? Can we change the gradual devolution of moral thinking that has gone on for decades and decades? Is this destruction or whatever truly going to happen, and why? Why am I so sure that something is going to happen? So, if I am sane, which is a debatable point, I realize there must be something we can do to change that future. If we cannot change anything, then at least we must warn the populace. So, Lloyd, my good nephew, if I am still playing with a full deck; there is darkness coming or some sort of devastation or derailment. Furthermore, it's coming in a twinkling, or at least pretty soon. Come Lloyd; we have much to do."

"Abbie, uh, Abraham, Uncle. We have to sit down and discuss this rationally. There is an amazing opportunity here that we are letting slip through our fingers. You are talking nonsense."

"Listen to me, Lloyd. There is no time for talk nor time for greed. We have a job to do, and we're on a mission! I hope it will be mission possible."

"Look, Abraham, you sound a little bit crazy. No, that, of course, is like saying Everest is a little high. You are in a bad way, Uncle."

The Abbie and the Lloyd are still in the apartment, and the Lloyd is resisting leaving.

"Lloyd, you should talk. Have you heard about people in glass houses? I agree that it could appear I am slightly imbalanced in relation to our world today. Perhaps a few thousand years ago, it would have been different. In an ancient time, a miraculous time, a wondrous time, perhaps what has happened to me would have made more sense to you, Lloyd, and maybe, more importantly, to me. Right now, sounding like some nutty prophet shouting from the mountaintops or whatever is really very inconvenient. Having said that, however, I have experienced something unusual and must follow through. But enough of that. I believe you have some things to explain."

"What do I have to explain? You have to do the explaining."

"Well, I'm not going to do the splaining around here, Bobbalouie. So, can you splain just how I disposed of the two gentlemen who were calling on you this afternoon? By the way, Lloyd, that sort of talk is from a very old cartoon that I saw. It is from the 1900s."

"I can't even think how you might have done that. Some form of hypnotism?"

"I'll do the thinnin' around here, Bobbalouie. Actually, Lloyd, you're not too far off. It's really a matter of stimulation of most of the afferent receptors innervating the surface of the skin all at once. It really amounts to information overload. This seldom happens normally, but it does occur when small animals become frozen or apparently so when attacked and cornered. People even used to feel that when, for a while, they were sticking themselves with needles or they used electric stimulation to attempt to decrease pain. But that was mostly hocus pocus, and a powerful placebo effect, although it was called a particular name, which I cannot remember. It showed the power of mental thought over physical pain. If you believe in something enough, you can numb yourself to pain. But that is enough regarding nerve stimulation. Anyway, your friends will recover in time. However, the reason that I want you to speculate about my little trick is to realize that it is something that I could not have previously done. I have changed, Lloyd. I have a certain presence with me. I possess knowledge that I shouldn't harbor."

"You mean someone present here besides me?"

Lloyd is obviously disturbed by the Abbie's statement and is pacing the floor.

"Yes, and I also have a certainty of belief, a conviction, that L.A. and San Fran will be destroyed, or at least changed, or radically altered. It is our mission to warn people of this fate. I don't know if we can reverse or change the future as I see it and redeem the cities, but if we can't, people must be alerted. Yep, Lloyd, it's 'save the cities time.' That is our immediate mission, our job, our assignment."

"Okay, Abraham. I don't know how you pulled your trick on these guys, but you seem to be waffling in and out of some type of trance. You are my uncle, and for all you've done for me, I'll listen. But how and why should the cities be destroyed? No meteorologist or scientist has predicted any new quake or tidal wave or nothing that I'm aware of. The lords of medicines and the news corps have a pretty good hold on the populace, and I don't think there will be any uprising. Hell, these aren't the worst cities in the world, and these aren't the worst times. In fact, we have more equality today than ever before. We have total freedom of expression and government, and with enough will, making the right deals, and greasing the right palms, anyone can do anything. I'll admit that total freedom comes at some price. It does make law and order a little difficult to interpret, and the police are non-existent, but we can basically do anything we want as long as we know the game and who the players are. No government controls us now, that's for sure."

"Yes, anything as long as you know the right people and you grease the right palms or have the power to order or convince people to do your bidding, as you say."

"Well, Uncle, I'll admit it might have allowed power groups to grow, but they don't bother most of us at all. We have real freedom. No more CIA, FBI. Remember the stories and the way the government controlled the people, the way they ran everything."

"I give you the fact that the power brokers are more open now than they used to be, but that doesn't seem to allow for any checks and balances. As long as you get along with the particular pharaoh in your area and pay your dues, you can prosper, although if you get too wealthy, you might attract some unwanted attention. The freedom to commercially sell drugs did help some aspects of the economy, and some of the poor, but the inability to have laws that stand for anything, resulted in the gradual dissolution of civilization. We no longer care for our people. There was a time the country, when it was a country, was clashing over universal medical care. Now there is no battle; everything seems to have gone, and it's gone in the name of individual freedom. Individuals or groups have triumphed, and as a result, there is no such thing as society, just individuals. We have made a giant step backward for humankind. There's no paternalism, no materialism, no nothing. We no longer have a society that cares for the group, and we, therefore, cannot care for the individual.

But I still don't know the mechanism of the destruction of the cities, and if there is some sort of cosmic explanation for the catastrophe, Lloyd, it certainly is not obvious to me. Having said all that, I have healed a bullet hole in my side, and you saw that yourself. Doom will happen. I've tried to reason with myself, tried to argue with my second self on the intrinsic quality of life, the innocence of so many people. Suppose there are 50 good people, or 40, 30, 20, even 10. Can anything justify killing or hurting all those people? I do believe that the system is wrong, and the people no longer really live. They have no meaning to their lives. Why, they are not even evolving. There is ultimate stagnation. Somehow the people must awaken, must look for common good, and develop a morality. Hey, this is good stuff, Lloyd. Why don't you record all these thoughts?"

The Abbie bangs his hand on the table and passes to the Lloyd a thin object, which in the Abbie's mind is called a tablet.

"Anyhow, somehow or other, we must show the people the way, or this local experiment will abort. So that is our mission. We need simple terminology which we can write in bold letters across a computer screen. For now, it's still STP, 'save the people.' It seems reasonable to save as many people as we can; perhaps a change will happen in the populace as we spread the word. The human population must wake up and save themselves. How many is many, I ask myself. You may note I often speak to myself and can carry on quite a dialogue. Do you ever carry on face-to-face conversations with yourself, Lloyd? I must make myself hold the rudder and not unravel, stay the course. I am in charge of my own brain and my own body.

How many need to be counted in order to halt the darkness, millions, thousands, tens, less than ten, one? Oh, what the hell am I talking about!"

Merge.

This host has not been controlled, as the others have, and this may lead to danger for this host. However, he has energy and a vision, which should help us. He, too, has almost died. We must not lose this host. We also must let him act, for the most part, on his own energy.

Submerge again.

"Abraham, this is incredible, not for believing! Do you really think God, Himself, or Herself, or whatever, is speaking to you? If he is, where the hell has He been up to now? He coulda helped a lot before now. You must be on something good to believe this shit. What a high!"

"I don't know where he has been, Lloyd. Perhaps he was sitting on the Throne of Mercy rather than of Justice. Lloyd, I've taken a temporary lapse of mind here. I don't even know if I am forming the words coming out of our mouths. What I do know is that we need to act quickly if we hope to get people out."

"Abraham, you're just plain crazy, and I'm not going along with this. I mean, you sound absolutely ridiculous. Someone is talking to you, God, or whoever. You'll never convince anyone of anything other than that you are nuts, and you'll never get anyone to leave the cities, not even me."

"Mmm, do you have a dictionary? No, never mind, we don't have time. Come over here, Lloyd, let me shake your hand, and I'll bid your present state adieu."

"Look, Uncle, you have treated me well and brought us out of the old place when I couldn't fend for myself. I hate to disappoint you, but let's shake hands and good luck to . . ."

The Abbie reaches out and shakes the hand of the Lloyd. We can feel him reaching in. He has learned how to do this without us!

"Ya know, Uncle, your hand feels so strange! The whole thing is becoming clearer to me. Where will we all go, Abraham? I will follow you anywhere!"

"You see, you just had a touching experience. It shows that you can only reach out and touch someone if you are actually there.

So, there is really nothing like being there. Televiewing doesn't do it. We are going to wend our way to Winnipeg. Now that you're on board, me mate, let's sail on over to visit the captain of this frigate and see if I can make him fathom the danger to the people so that he will forewarn them and flag the Titanic problem."

"You'll be able to convince him, Abraham; you convinced me."

"I was able to convince you with my touch. Energy from within me entered you and changed some patterns in your brain. I just turned the right switches and that convinced you. I am not sure what would have happened if you were really opposed to what I wanted you to believe. Perhaps you would have frozen like our friends over there. I can do this without fully understanding how I do it, or if someone else is doing it for me, you know, that visitor I may have."

"Yes, but Abbie, you, unfortunately, can't go around touching several million people."

"You're right, Lloyd. I'll have to endeavor to use my electric and persuasive oratorical power. Despite the adjectives, that part of my capacity has never had much of a jolt in it. I know that this whole thing sounds preposterous, but there is this other sense, yes, that's it, another sense, a sixth one, that keeps whispering to me to continue my course. This is despite the fact that it is impossible to accomplish if not totally loco."

"Abraham, it is you who has the Divine Knowledge, but I do have an idea as to how to spread the Word."

"Lloyd, my nephew, I don't know anything about divine knowledge, although I do seem to have some sort of prescience. I'll give you that— the whole thing is strange. I wake up one morning with more than a purpose on my mind. I have a sense of impending doom and a mission to fulfill, for who or what, I don't know. The other thing I don't know is whether I can convince people of this mission. Oh, well, maybe if I'm not number one, I will just have to try harder."

"I don't quite get your meaning, but I will try to understand."

"Oh, there is no great meaning here, Lloyd. In order to better understand me, you just have to be more facile with old commercials. Don't worry about it. So how do you think we should spread the vision? You said you had an idea."

"Uncle, in order to reach the people, we just have to put it on the net, do Facebook, chats, etc. It should be a snap."

"I dunno, Lloyd. There are a million of these pronouncements on various areas of the net. No one actually believes them anymore, and they won't make people seek safety even if a raging forest fire like they used to have is upon them."

"Then, Abbie, speak to the communicators. They're the people who think, make, and report the news. They control all the media. They still have enormous influence in some quarters."

"There's an idea, Lloyd. I think that might work even though reporting has increasingly become more inventive than investigative. We have never solved the problem of combining a free communication system, uncontrolled reporting, and responsibility in the journalism industry. It's representation by what might sell, or what the reporter happens to think, feel, or wish."

"It is not a bad system, Abbie. It's basic commercialism and the way people get their say. If they make you want the product, then you do want it."

"Possibly, Lloyd, it is the epitome of freedom after all. But the development of communications has given the communicators unparalleled power. Never have our inputs been so totally controlled, and never before have we depended on electrical media so much to give us all our knowledge. There may be a true freedom in that, but it has progressively lost its meaning, with the only responsibility that the media has is an internal one. Unfortunately, there is no universal morality test for them or anyone else. There are no moral controls, and morality is a societal thing. We should have a democratic system to determine the moral norm of the particular society, and reporting should not necessarily augment the moral standard but reveal its biases. Yep, there should be democratic reporting. Every four years or so, or five, we should put up the commandments of the society and vote on them, and everything should flow from that. I know there are some problems there, but hey, I've only been working on this for a few days.

Just stop me when I continue to run off at the mouth, Lloyd. I just seem to have so many ideas crammed inside my head these days. You know this has happened to me before."

"What is the meaning of your statements, Uncle?"

"Oh, I just mean that the media have complete control of the news but have only to represent themselves and make sure they get sponsorship. Suppose, however, they had to represent a constituency, such as some politicians used to do, or more precisely, if they had to utilize the moral ideas of the populace, provided we did that in some democratic way. Then the media would have to report the same matters with the bias of their constituency rather than their own bias, or perhaps openly represent the people that have their bias. If they had to report that they were representative of this group or faction, then at least their reports would be placed on that background which would be more on the up and up. Now, how would an evolution of change happen to that society? Would there still be influences? Yep, I think so. Understand, Lloyd, I think it's coming."

"I don't know, Abbie. Why would that system be better than the present system?"

The Abbie is trying to think now about how to make a new society. This is the plan. He is pacing back and forth as he is thinking.

"Well, Lloyd, then you would clearly know who the communicator represented; one could then read or hear about it with that in mind and balance against the bias, against their commandments. Also, since somewhere the beliefs of that group would have to be stated, one would know in detail beforehand the backgrounds of the reporters. For instance, it would be like your, or at least my belief in a science story, as given to me by someone with some type of journalistic degree versus someone who had a background in science. One comes with some knowledge, one with a lot, but both have a set of standards. Nowadays, those two are represented as equal opinions."

The Lloyd and the Abbie have finally left the apartment and are walking toward the Emats as the Abbie continues to talk.

"As I think about it, however, I'm on a roll here, but the whole system would not work because the journalist would lie about his standards or morals, and it would be too restrictive. Rival underground communicators would undoubtedly arise since they would feel the system did not represent them, and then there would be an attempt to suppress them. Any underground system would appear to be less associated with normative politics, and many people like to go against the norms. Therefore, the power of the unrepresentative or non-moral system would gain prominence. That might result in the same system as we have now, where the reporters or communicators, with little knowledge and huge unstated values, would report from their own bias. So, I have set up, in my mind's eye, a normative society, a moral society, based on the people's desires, only to have it come crashing to the ground. I wonder how long it would take to unwind. Maybe in the interim, there would be some golden age. A revolution that might, at least transiently, make it all worthwhile. We might inch forward in our civilization. Lloyd, I am just trying various scenarios in my mind's eye. There is too much control by the media who really do not necessarily have any moral guidance other than their own bias."

"Uncle?"

The Abbie is wrapped up in ideas that are coming fast and does not apparently hear the Lloyd.

"It is not the best, and indubitably not even the worst of times. The times are simply an evolution, partly as a result of our massive, all-pervasive communication system and a loss of clear guidelines as to how we should live our lives. Any path is possible and acceptable, all right and wrong at the same time. We have to accept societies and practices while establishing ethical norms. Is that what this is all about? Is that something I'm supposed to do?"

The Abbie is beginning to realize the work that is in his future.

The Lloyd is confused.

"Uncle, what about all the new technology that has been developed? People adopted it, and the climate has stabilized, although a bit wild." Maybe this will help us."

"Perhaps new technology will allow change in some future time, with direct input from the populace. However, that never worked with the internet. New technology will facilitate a change in society only if another group with a particular mission gains control of the technologies, and then there has to be a wide, almost universal input and accepted. That is what happened with climate change although even there some of the change had to be with a whip rather than the feather. Any overarching moral ground rules would still affect some adversely. How could it not? How can all people with differing moral and ethical codes be treated the same by a benign entity? They can't. There must always be some losers. Is that a lesson? Who is good, and who is evil? Are there any such definitions? What the hell am I talking about, anyhow? Do you have any idea, Lloyd?

"Well, right now we have to try to save some lives or something like that."

"I am trying to understand but having a hard time. "So, what are we to do, Abraham?"

"We are to try to use whatever system we can to save millions of lives. Seems like a reasonable thing to do. What my palaver was all about was simply my ruminations on the new society and how we would try to construct it or how someone or something else might construct it. Can one have a universal world society? Are we all just hard-wired in the wrong way? I haven't got a clue as to what to do, just as you suggested, Lloyd."

"I am truly honored that you have taken my opinion into account, Uncle."

"Don't be honored, be honest. Come, let's hit the communicators and see if we can at least complete that part of the task. Let's get the communicators to really perform a service to the people."

"Uncle, you said, 'Be honest, not honored.' What a meaningful statement! We will carry that forward."

"Lloyd, I think I changed you just a little too thoroughly. I didn't mean to completely erase that lovable nasty part of your personality. Let's just carry ourselves forward to the communicators, and we will set out the whole story before them. We will tell them my fears for the cities and see if we can get any buy-in. Perhaps they will think it crazy enough that they will give it some publicity, and they do have influence. We're off to see the damn communicators of San. Can we get them to tell and to save everyone from hell? And now the chorus, we're off to see the dam, communicators of San."

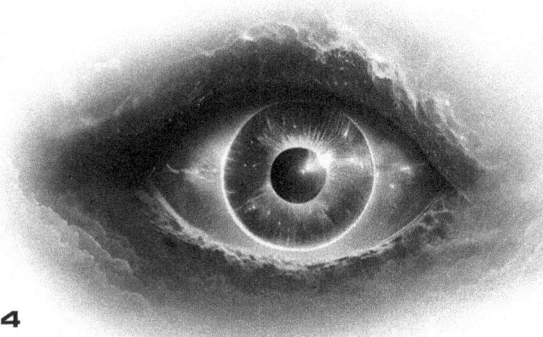

CHAPTER 14

The Communicators

The Abbie and the Lloyd approach a large building with a glowing sign that says World Wide News Network, WWNN, San Francisco Branch.

"Lloyd, so this is the temple of the communicators. Impressive! The god of sensation must truly be a powerful god."

"There shalt be no other gods before me! Abraham, you know that!"

"I'm just being facetious, Lloyd. Don't get your toga in a tangle. How did I make you so damn religious anyhow? What or how did I do that? Why do I not worry about that more than I do? That in itself is a worry. Well, let's just play this out. Keep the eye on the game, and maybe somehow, the rest of life will straighten out. Maybe Seri's right. I could be crazy, but then how did I do what I did to Lloyd and those two guys in Frisco? Oh, well, to the job at hand.

I wonder how we can get to the top of the editorial staff, the guys that have the clout?"

"God will provide a way, Abraham."

"Mmm, that's very helpful, Lloyd. I wonder if I can put some type of reverse touch on you to bring you back to life. Oh, well, in balance, you're probably improved.

I guess the best way to get to the top is to try the honest approach first. We simply walk in and tell the communicators at WWNN that we have a wonderful but frightening, incredible story, which I know about because I happen to be prescient. Seems logical, no?"

"I guess so, Uncle. Will they believe you?"

"We are doing this to save a whole bunch of people, and the newsmakers could be of help. Hopefully, they can report the story in a truthful but catchy fashion, which could influence the masses. They certainly know how to influence people."

"Yeh, but Abbie, can you influence these influencers to tell the story? Good joke, huh?"

"Oh, yes, it should be a snap. The only slight problem is the fact that the story is fantastic and unbelievable. Somehow or other, we have to make them believe in the danger. No, that's probably irrelevant. Somehow or other, we have to make the newsmakers believe that the prediction is newsworthy and will capture the public's fancy for a day or two, so more of them will pay to tune into the communicators. The veracity of the story has little to do with whether we can get this out to the public. We have to make them believe that the story will attract viewers."

"The inspiration will come, Abraham, have faith, and it will be there. It is all in the hands of the great one, and He will show you the way. I now know this to be true, Abraham!"

"I can't tell you how helpful these deep insights are, Lloyd. I wonder what I inscribed on your brain. Just keep coming up with those wonderful ideas. I wonder if my touch will wear off. And what about that touch, Abraham, old boy? You've become one weird fellow, and yet it doesn't seem to bother me. I should be running around saying I've changed. I must be dreaming, so go lie down. But every time I try to touch those feelings and describe what's happening to me, something just shuts off up there in my head. I almost begin to feel calmer even now, even though I cannot make any sense of what has become of me. Soothed and calmed."

The Abbie and the Lloyd are walking up to the WWNN building and are about to enter. They look and are impressed with the beautiful gardens and lawns surrounding the building.

"Do you mind going through those doors first, Lloyd? Recently, I have had trouble with doors, so I will sneak in behind you."

"No problem, Unc. Trouble with doors?"

"I will explain later."

"You know, it's as if someone has rerouted my brain circuits. I'm calmed, and I don't try to read into my own mind."

"Well, let's take stock, Lloyd. Here we are in San Francisco, guided by a prescient conviction that something disastrous will happen to L.A. and this town. When I just let it all hang out like that, it leaves me with no uncertainty as to whether I should go back to see the shrink, Dr. Naivir. What's happening to me, Lloyd? What's happening to the old white (well, not so white, I guess), haired professor here?"

"What exactly do you mean, Uncle?"

"Well, am I me, and if not, where did 'me' go? I am me. There is definitely 'a me' inside my head, but there is more than just me, Lloyd. Believe it or not, my nose is more sensitive. I can remember smells, scents, the sweet smell of the woodlands. My recognition of smells and my sensitivity to them is remarkably increased. My mind has gained memories, Lloyd. I remember intimate details of people that I've never met. I don't remember being struck by lightning. Maybe I was hit, and it rearranged some circuitry. Who is Ike? He's a boy lost in the wilderness alone with his mother. He is almost like a son to me, at least in terms of my feelings towards him. I have to help Ike make an Emats. He's not exactly in a wilderness; he's somewhere in what were the northern states with his mother, Helen. Who is Helen, my wife? I have a wife, but her name is Seri.

I have memories of a forest, a wolf pack, and another partner there. You know, I may have another son, except this one is a wolf. I also have a desire to have a dog to run in the forest with. Sounds reasonable, no? Is this creature my offspring? I can just see a book, *The Offspring*. Boy, that is chilling. You know, I even have a vague recollection of some other strange life form."

"Another life form, Abbie?"

"Yes, it may have been extraterrestrial. I or it was flying on a planet something like ours, but not the same.

The growth was abundant and huge in proportion to what it is on our earth. The life forms were different, all of them. They are all giants compared to Earth, the colors brighter and some that I cannot place, So I must have seen something on some other planet, or as usual, I have a very vivid imagination. No, that's not it. It was a bee, and I can smell out nectar because of that experience. I saw things through the eye of a bee!

What is happening to me? Why do I have these thoughts? I MUST be going nuts!"

"Abraham, are you speaking to me? Are you okay? You said something to me, and then you kind of got glassy-eyed and started muttering to yourself. I started talking to you, and you stopped muttering. Snap out of it!"

"I don't know what's the matter, Lloyd, my confused but faithful nephew. Yeh, I'm fine, Lloyd, in a very bewildered sort of way. I think my noggin' is playing some tricks on me. Something is wrong with this strange man who is me. Perhaps I have tilted at windmills too many times, the idols of our society. So many have called me crazy. Perhaps I'm beginning to believe it.

No, I was just thinking about why I'm thinking and actually following through on all these preposterous thoughts. I have been exploring my own mind, Lloyd, and after due consideration, have come to the conclusion that I'm even nuttier than I thought I was at casual examination. Well, I'll have to think about that and all my far-away progeny or whatever they are at another time, in another space, where maybe I can put some of this together. Seri will help me. She always helps put things into the proper perspective, or at least one I have not thoroughly considered. Lloyd, let's go to the reception desk of WWNN since we have entered the building. We will gain entrance to the inner sanctum of the newsmakers, alias the communicators."

The Abbe and the Lloyd walk over to a desk marked Reception. A young woman with reddish hair is sitting behind the desk. She is at the computer. The floors are shiny and not made of wood but a type of stone. Pictures of mostly men hang on the walls, with some paintings which are not realistic and must be the abstract paintings we read about.

"Greetings Ms., or should I call you Joy Traaverse? We would be highly honored if we could speak to the editorial staff. My name is Abraham Benterah. I come, originally, from the city of Ur of Kengir, then Amurru."

The receptionist looks up and has what must be a puzzled look on her face. Her eyes are brown.

"Abraham, what are you talking about? How did you know her name? You become more fantastic every minute. You have been touched. God is truly wondrous, and you are truly his friend. He works in mysterious ways, and all will be wonderful if we follow in his ways!"

"As far as her name is concerned, Lloyd, I managed that little trick by reading the flasher on her desk. As far as that city of origin business, I'm not quite sure. That just came out of my mouth, from my own little corrugated brain. Just one more of those short circuits I've been telling you about. Funny, though, the perception that I do come from where I said I did, even though you and I know I come from the Middle East or what used to be the Middle East. I dunno. I dunno, Lloyd. Perhaps you're right; maybe God is greater than I think."

"God is everywhere, Abraham!"

"Gentlemen, do you have an appointment?"

"We would like to see the editor, Ms. Traaverse, or we would like to traverse these halls in search of a joyful editor. Or, Joy Traaverse, joyfully traverse us to . . ."

"And which of the editors do you wish to see?"

"Well, Joy, if I may call you that, since I have done so already, I am not sure which of the learned folks I wish to see, but I have what could be literally an earthshaking story. Who is the head man, the chieftain of this city?"

"Mr. Kenterah, is that your name? I'm afraid it's impossible to see any of the editors today, especially Mr. Hurrian, without an appointment. It's simply impossible. If you have an interesting story, you can find an investigative reporter. If they like your story well enough, they will have access to the editors. Firstly, please let me imprint your palm to make sure you have the right type of clearance to be seen. Thank you, you have had considerable controversial publicity in the past. You took part in marches holding signs that indicated many news organizations, especially WWNN, was not telling the truth. I think you may have destroyed some of our property. You appear to like upsetting some of the fine people of our conglomerate. Nonetheless, there is no ban on you seeing a reporter noted in the computer."

"Joy, me girl. Would you not speak to Mr. Hurrian on the visor and just tell him of an incredible story that I will reveal to him alone?"

"Well, as I already said, I can see if there are any of the investigative reporters around and if they will listen to your story. Tell me the meat of the story."

"Well, let me hold your hand as I relate it to you so I can help with the indescribable shock that might occur as I reveal this to you. I can assure you that you will be touched by this revelation."

The person Joy has reached out her hand to the Abbie, looking at him strangely. The Abbie was able to make her do that. We do not know how. There, he has reached in.

"There, that's better. This city and the City of Angels will be destroyed through a natural or perhaps unnatural, or perhaps even a mystical but nonetheless catastrophic event unless, somehow, I can stop it. Seems reasonable, no? Now, I am sure that you will have someone direct us to the office of Mr. Bale Hurrian, the big-time newsmaker."

The Joy is now calm and smiles. The Abbie has made the changes in her brain.

"Of course, I will, and may the Lord be with you as he always is and will ever be, Abraham. I will get Clive, our runner. He shows people around and also delivers certain things to the offices if we do not wish the robots to drive them.

"Clive, direct these gentlemen right up to the office of Mr. Hurrian. I'll call him that they're coming. They are important, Clive. They bring us a message, a true message. Something is again going to change this world. Oh, Abraham, I am so happy you have come again. Is it starting all over? Is that the message?"

"Okay, Jojo. Clive is here to give you cheer. Oh, yeah, so have no fear, and blah, blah, blah. Hey there, Jo, are you sure I should take them up there, in the thin air? Is it all right with the cruelers, our very own rulers?"

The Clive is a tall man with black, very curly hair. He is taller than the Lloyd, and his skin is darker. He does not look threatening.

"Go, Clive. I know this is the right thing to do. Oh, Abraham, in case you hadn't guessed, Clive is a Rhymer."

"Thank you, Joy or Jojo, if you prefer. I haven't met many Rhymers. By the way, if this meeting is unsuccessful, or even if I convince them to print the story, yeh, in either instance, I suggest you take an early vacation. The holiday should be as far away from this city as you can readily get. And I'd go soon, very soon."

"Thank you, Abraham. Where should I go?"

"Well, many of us are going to wend our way to Winnipeg, but I'm not sure how long the journey will take. You are welcome to come, as are you, Clive. The important thing is to absent yourself from California."

"Wend to Winnipeg, Abraham. As it is stated, so it shall be done! Let's take the dive."

"Thank you, Lloyd. I'm not sure why my touch on you had such a pile-driving effect. I wonder if it will wear off and you will return to your senses? On the other hand, maybe this is a better condition for you to be in."

"By the way, Abbie, what's a Rhymer?"

"I don't know much about them except what Google knowledge tells me. A religious sect that believes that nature is in rhythm with all life. To develop and maintain health and happiness, one needs to discover the music, the rhythm of nature, and the environment. A mechanism to achieve that is to adjust the cadence of your body movement and your speech to the surroundings. The speech is best aligned with the present environment and nature by a simple rhyme. That's the sum total of my knowledge.

It must be newer than the dictionary I perused. No matter, lead on McClive. Let us not tarry to the Hurrian. We must hurry."

"You got it, Abraham, my man. You sound like one crazy dude to me, but that fits me to a tee. We'll take the pneumatic all the way to the attic. It's all the way up to 44. Let me show you the pneumatic door. What's a Winnipeg, don't make me beg?"

They all walk together through a relatively narrow part of the building that must be called a hall. The floor is made of the same shiny stone. Pictures are hanging on the walls, mostly of men, although some women are shown. Some pictures or paintings are not realistic. They walk toward some doors that look like elevator doors but are called pneumatic—there must be some difference.

"Clive, Winnipeg is a dying city in the east of Wescan bordering the country of Ontario, built on an old fur trading route at the junction of the Red and Assiniboine Rivers. It's also near the shores of several large shallow inland lakes of glacial origin. The land surrounding the city used to flow with milk and especially bread, with some honey, I suppose. It is a land of severity, severe winters and summers. They have wild mosquitoes that are supposed to be able to drain a man's blood in twenty minutes in the wilderness unless you apply a chemproof. It is becoming more obscure and forgotten daily and is no longer the center of trade and commerce it was over a few centuries ago. It is a developing wasteland. No one wants to live there, and everyone wishes to leave. And, oh yes, I believe the future of our world, as we humans have a run at it, will revolve around its center at Portage and Main. Long live Portage and Main."

"You're one weird man, Abraham. Here we be. Hey, there, Sandy, sweet, take these men to Hurrian to meet. Sandy is Hurrian's exec, and she plays with a full deck."

"I don't have anything about a meeting scheduled for Mr. Hurrian, Clive."

The Abbie is looking intently at the yellow-haired exec. She is mid-aged and has a very determined look on her face.

"Well, Sandy, sweet. Jojo sent me up, and I don't mean to be crude; she said that it was okay with the Hurrian dude."

"Well, good for her, but there is nothing on the computer, so I can't understand why she would be under that impression. Let me see, no; there is definitely nothing here. I can't let them in. Hurrian would be furious. Now, Clive, get them out of here, or Hurrian will have our jobs."

"Excuse me, Sandy, but let me see for myself. This appointment was set up just as this computer went offline for some reason. At least, I think that is what Jo mentioned. I don't know much about these thinking computers, but perhaps this appointment was set up before this computer was online or before any computer was online. As a matter of fact, I believe it must have been set up ages and ages ago."

The Abbie has turned the screen towards him, but the Sandy turns it back.

"What is your name, sir?"

"I am Abraham Benterah, and this is my nephew, Lloyd Benach. I am pleased to make your acquaintance."

"There is no appointment here for either of you, and the computer has told me that no other appointment has been made by anyone for you or even a name resembling yours at least in the last year. Since all the appointments are logged on the internal net, there is no mistake. Now, I don't know what came over Joy, but there is no reason for us to have any further discussion. Mr. Hurrian is engaged in a meeting at this time and has no time to see anyone. I am sorry if this is an inconvenience, but next time if you make an appointment beforehand, you may be able to see him. Good day, gentlemen. Clive, throw them out."

"Such assurance and decision-making are hard to find in people these days. Let me shake your hand, and we shall thereafter obey your every wish and command."

"Here is my hand; there is the pneumatic. Take them, Clive . . ."

Cosmic Eyes

The Joy points to the pneumatic and does not wish to touch the Abbie's hand, but the Abbie grabs her pointing finger. She is speaking.

"I see everything! He is, as He is, He is everywhere!"

"So he is, or she is, and everything is beautiful. I believe our appointment with Mr. Hurrian now exists. Do you wish to send us in?"

"That wish is beyond dispute. Your appointment has always existed, for thousands of years, from the beginning of time!"

"From the beginning of time? I do believe in booking ahead or you may not get a good table. Booking it at the beginning of time seems like pushing it just a bit. However, I guess you cannot be too careful. Why do people I touch get so overblusen with religion? What vibes am I giving out anyway? All I try to do is reach in and bring down the resistance, and yet it seems like I am hitting them with a hammer. What am I? Who am I? Abbie, baby, how can you do these things? Where did I get the knowledge? Who is up there in your brain with you anyway?"

"Abraham, why are you tapping your head like that? Shouldn't we go to see the editor now?"

"Yeh, we should, Lloyd. We might as well play this out and see where it goes. By the way, Sandy, I would visit Winnipeg in the very near future or at the very least, leave the city. I would put many, many miles and even more kilometers between you and this once-fair city. Do that in the next week, Sandy. This is a very solemn warning. It is important that you leave. Do you understand?"

The Sandy appears to be very happy; she is smiling, and her eyes are bright and yet there are some tears. She touches the wire attached to her earphone and speaks to it.

"Mr. Hurrian, I have two very important men, you must see. An appointment was made a long time ago. It's funny. It seems the appointment was made a very long time ago but was somehow overlooked. Will you see them now, sir, please!"

"What's eating you, Sandy? I don't see anything on the computer. I gave you explicit instructions that I was not to be disturbed today. This is not like you. Just rebook the damned appointment. Are your earphones on, Sandy? They're not listening to any of this, are they?"

"The earphones are on, Mr. Hurrian."

"Good. Who are these men and is there any danger? Answer evasively if there is."

"It's a Mr. Benterah and a Mr. Benach. There is nothing to suggest that there is anything to fear as I read it, sir. I would not think there is any chance. The feeling I have is wonder. They have astonishing news to tell you."

"Yeh, I'm sure. Benterah, Benach, nope doesn't ring any bells. Never heard of them. The names sound Jew. Are they dressed funny, you know, with long beards and stuff? Ah, to hell with them; just rebook the appointment. If it were anything really important, one of the reporters would have spoken to them and me. Forget about booking anything with me; make the appointment with one of the reporters. Whatever they have to tell us can be sorted out with one of our investigators. Now don't bother me with any more nonsense!"

"They're not dressed funny, Mr. Hurrian, although both have beards, but kinda nice ones. They're not wearing any funny hats or anything, though. Please, Mr. Hurrian, oh . . ."

"From your hesitation, Sandy, it appears that Mr. Hurrian is incredibly anxious to see us. Just show us to the right door, Clive, and we'll just let ourselves in. We really do not have to wait for him to issue a formal invitation or to escort us. No use standing on ceremony with old, old friends like us."

"I don't know, Abe. What you did to my Sandy babe. You mesmerize, hypnotize? Look Abraham, let's just go, and I find you an investigator foe. I do not want to tangle with you, your pal but especially Mr. Bal. Ya gotta bow down to that son of a bitch 'cause he has more power than a witch."

"I understand, Clive. Just show us the door and disappear. We'll make our way without you here. We won't tell Bal Hurrian of your service, so no cause for you to be nervous."

"Savvy, go left, down the hall, that second hanging on the wall. On the right is an entrance way; it's controlled with some type of ray. Or a code from the outside will open it, but I don't know it, no shit. While you're trying to get inside, I'm off to save my very own hide."

The Clive rushes off down the hall. He appears to be quite frightened of the Hurrian.

"Here we are, Lloyd. The entrance way has an electric lock, but I believe it won't give me a shock. Clive's gone. I guess I can stop that now. Hmm, let's take a close look at this lock. Yep, I can interfere with it. Inactivating it will allow the damn thing to open Here we go, Lloyd. I believe the game is afoot. Let's see where I'll, or whoever is guiding me, take us."

The Lloyd and the Abbie enter the office. A large white-haired man is sitting behind a large desk. His face is scowling, and he is looking into the screen on his desk. The chairs in the room opposite the desk have very thick seats. There is a large painting behind him which appears to be a characterization of himself, although he appears thinner in the picture with black and white hair.

"Mr. Hurrian, sir. I'm Abe Benterah, and this is my nephew and follower, Lloyd Benach. So happy that we can see you. Can I call you Bal?"

"What the hell! How in the fuck did you get in here?"

The Hurrian touches a button on his shirt pocket.

"Sandy, send the enforcers now! I have a gun on you, Abe, or whatever you said your name was, and the enforcers will be here in about one minute. You may turn around and walk out as quickly and as quietly as you came, and I may not turn them on you if you're very lucky!"

"I've already been fatally shot once today, and do not relish that experience again. I think it was touch and go, as they say. Come to think of it, I'm not even sure how I survived that particular event. I can assure you Mr. Hurrian, that we mean you no harm. We would have acted immediately if we were truly assassins since we were able to enter your office undetected. Therefore, we are not hired killers. In any event, we are to be forced out of here in a minute or two. I'll at least tell why we took all this trouble to break in here. Your world, and that of L.A., is going to be darkened or eliminated in the near future by a cataclysm. It is important to get that news out as effectively as possible to the people. It also has to be done in an orderly manner so that a methodical evacuation can be planned. If you promise to put that on home video, we will leave immediately. I'm not sure exactly when this will happen, but it will be soon."

The Hurrian jumps up from behind his desk and waves the weapon around. This poses a threat as the Abbie has almost been killed once.

"That's it? That's your news? Another end-of-the-world pronouncement, which you want me, as a responsible news provider, to put that nonsense out on our electronic mediums. Can you imagine the terror that would produce if we did it? The havoc it would cause just because you strolled in here and asked for it? At least some of the assholes in the street are able to pick the date of destruction. You can't even do that! Get the fuck out of here! Where the hell are the enforcers! Sandy! What the hell's going on!"

"I don't think Sandy called the enforcers for you. I drugged her, and she is a little touched right now. How can I prove to you that I know what I'm talking about? I have some powers; do you have a dictionary?"

"What? A dictionary! Look, you pimpish idiot fucknose! Get out of my office, or I will shoot! I'll call the enforcers myself!"

"Oh, Abbie, he does not believe in the Everlasting One. Do not raise false gods in front of Him. It will anger him. He is already angry."

"Thank you, Lloyd. That should help a bundle. Look, Mr. Hurrian, despite the vacuous verblings of my nephew here, he does have a point. I know something is going to happen, and millions will die, at least I think that is the case, if we do not intervene. Please listen! There must be a way I can convince you. Would you alert someone to have the San Andrea fault checked? Can you run an earthquake predictor? We must do something!"

"I'll believe you when it happens, and it's not going to happen. This is not a story. This is pure bullshit."

"Okay, I've seldom met a man as self-assured as you are. You also claim prescience over my foretelling. Let me shake your hand, sir, and I will do whatever you subsequently wish me to do."

"Take another step forward and you'll get my wish right between the eyes. I may do it anyway, in view of the inconvenience you have caused me."

"I'm on my way, sir. Please excuse me. You're unlikely to hear from me again. Let's go, Lloyd. Something tells me we're not wanted."

"Abraham, why do we leave? He did not listen to your words!"

"You wins some; you loses some. Speaking of which, I think the enforcers have arrived."

Two large men enter the room. One has no hair on his head. Their muscles are seen through their tight shirts. They look angry.

"You two, take these men, this Abraham shit, and show them why they should have manners around Communicative headquarters in the future!"

The Hurrian is waving his gun, directing the enforcers towards the Abbie and the Lloyd, but stays behind his desk.

"Yes, sir, Mr. Hurrian! Come on over here, you shit. Don't make me get blood on this nice carpet."

The men have pushed the Abbie and the Lloyd out of the room and into the pneumatic. They push them out the door of the building and toward a conveyance called a shooter.

"Now get into that shooter. He is with me forever and ever. I will follow!"

"Pete, what the fuck? Grab this guy's other hand. He is as He will be!!!"

"Thank you very much, gentlemen. What a shame that Mr. Hurrian did not get to see your sudden change of heart. It's amazing that even these ruffians have spirituality and probably superstition just below the surface. Too bad, oh, well. If Bal had seen this demonstration, he would probably have tried to shoot us all rather than reporting a wonderful event. I don't think it is worthwhile going back in there.

I am not sure he should actually want to report a preventative action that might actually save some people. He would get too much pleasure out of reporting the incident and acting as the observer rather than getting embroiled in the event. There is nothing like a little human sacrifice to make front-page news.

Pete, Harty, I am Abraham Benterah. Your expressions are much calmer and brighter than they were a few moments ago."

"I know who you are, oh, Abraham. I do feel so good, so full of life. Thank you, we'll do whatever you ask."

"So, I must transmit my name as well. A touch is worth much more than a picture but is not very satisfying. I'm scrambling people's brains, such as they are, and I'm not sure how I'm doing it. Is it worth making a bunch of reverent robots so I can accomplish whatever it is that I'm supposed to do? It doesn't feel right. It's certainly not subtle. If I knew what I did, I could control some of it, but it just comes when I want to accomplish something or when I am in big trouble."

"Here is the entrance, Abraham. God bless ya be both."

"Thank you both, and I would suggest that both of you take an extended vacation in the next week, or at least leave the Bay area and avoid L.A. Let me try to explain. I have this conviction that something terrible, a great darkness, is going to happen in both of these cities. I, for some strange reason, am tied up with it, and somehow, I think there is something I should do to stop it. It's a little difficult because I don't know if it's going to happen, what's going to happen, and what I am supposed to do to try and stop it. So, it's wise to clear out of town. I also have some type of date in Winnipeg, but that's another story. Got it?"

"Yessir. God is great."

Yes, Shalom Pete, Harty, and we'll see you in the future. Perhaps we'll see you on the way to Winnipeg. Let's go, Lloyd. There are some other lesser communicators, but I think we have shot the bolt here. Hurrian would not allow anything to go out now that we have made him so mad. Perhaps we will have a little more luck in L.A."

"How do you want to travel, Uncle? Emats Express, Zeppelin, or the old commuter airplane? You know, Abbie, I've got an idea. How about we get a bunch of these guys that you have convinced and go down to one of the newsmaker places with all of them and take over the place? Those guys that just almost threw us out would be good ones to enlist. Then maybe the newsmakers will believe you."

"Ten good people and true. Well, you may have something there, Lloyd. But I don't want to make any zombies, spouting the end of the world or God's will.

I would rather we actually convince people somehow or other. Well, let's work on it on the journey. Zeppelin sounds good. I feel we should be environmental in our present role. If we have trouble with wind or the heated upward drafts of the cities, perhaps I can touch the winds and make them hail God."

"You can do that!"

"Frankly, my dear nephew, since I do not know why I am doing what I am doing, and since when I do these things, I don't know how I do them, I really don't know what I can and can't do. It's getting a little discomforting. One thing I know for certain. I'll think at least a few minutes before frying anybody else's brain. I seem to be able to turn it on and off, but I'm not sure if there are more than just those two settings. Of course, then there is the little problem of what is going on and why am I doing all these crazy things!"

"Uncle Abbie, uh, Abraham, you sound troubled."

"Troubled . . . I wouldn't call myself troubled. I'd call it mild concern. All I've done is uproot my life, do things that I shouldn't be able to do, and know things I shouldn't know. Other than that, I'm not troubled. I am perhaps a little vexed. I'm vexed, Lloyd, peeved. Yes, a little peeved at what life has suddenly dealt me. I'm sailing into the wind, towards an unknown destination, in a vessel I know little about. I certainly cannot seem to come about, and I am having a great deal of difficulty in tacking. Why me? If it is some spirit that is sailing the boat, why did it pick on me?

Is someone or something else guiding my voyage? I just hope I can read the charts. No, Lloyd. I'm not peeved or vexed, just a little bit mad, Lloyd, and I haven't been at the mercury."

"Abbie, Abraham, you were always a little offbeat, but there was something you could always trust about you. Everyone felt that way about you. We know you're not perfect, but you had a charisma and integrity that everyone respected. I don't know if that helps since I didn't understand most of what you were just talking about."

"Lloyd, you sound a little more like yourself! That is good news. I never intended to change people permanently, or at least most of the time, although I do seem to remember some permanent changes that were purposefully inserted. I just don't know where I am going. I really may have a fixed delusion here, Lloyd. I hope that touch thing wears off people. So, Lloyd, am I talking to the real you now?"

The Lloyd is shaking his head. They are approaching a building that has a sign indicating Zeppelin Terminal.

"Yeh, I feel like I just woke up from one great week, but somehow, I can't describe it. I'm not quite the same. What did you do? Whatever it was, it sure made me feel different. I feel purpose in my life again.

I feel that there is a reason to live. Maybe there is something greater than us out there. Maybe there is reason and ration behind all this, and not a dice role. I think you convinced me."

"Well, I'm relieved that you are returning to your old self. It does make me feel a little less like a monster. At least I haven't changed people permanently.

Lloyd, can you describe to me what it was like."

"Well, a part of me seemed somewhat asleep. For a period of time there were certain things that I could see and feel clearly. Nothing else seemed to interfere with those feelings. They were paramount in all my thinking. I now feel like my old self now, pretty much, but something has changed."

"Changed? How changed, Lloyd?"

"Well, my feeling toward you seems kinda like mixed up. In the past, I always was sorta angry at you, as well as feeling close to you. You have been like an older brother to me since my own father died. Now, I'm clearly for you, and I don't seem to have any resentment left. I'm not as afraid as I used to be. You don't know some of the things that I have done in the past, even to my family. I don't think I would act like that anymore. I dunno, I just seem to have my life and priorities straightened out, at least much more than they used to be."

"Lloyd, I'm happy for you. But I've got to find out what's happening to me. I don't know if I like this magic touch. It might turn out to be the Midas massage. Let's park here, go into the Zeppelin terminal and float back to the L of A. I've got to save people or find ten good people true or at least get myself straightened out in the attempt."

"What do you mean, get yourself straightened out, Abraham?"

"Oh, nothing much. It's just that as far as I can figure, I'm possessed, as well as being bothered and bewildered, am I."

Merge.

Abraham is quite bothered by our presence, and he is the only host so far that has been conscious of the fact. He is lurching toward action. It is difficult to know if we should reveal ourselves in a more profound way in order to demonstrate that our presence is a reality. Conversely, he operates relatively well without too much interference. If we become more obvious, it may lead him to exterminate himself or cause others to try. Submerge.

"Uncle, Abbie, you were just speaking and then had one of your lapses. What were you talking about, Uncle?"

"Did I? Something was going on in my mind, a discussion without me. Am I berserk? There is a lot of evidence to suggest that except, except, I do have strange powers. Something has changed inside me, and I am not sure what. Perhaps there is a God.

Why on earth would he pick on me? Perhaps He didn't. Those memories I have were perhaps previous choices. Okay, it is what it is, even if I am going insane. Let us stay the course."

Sorry, Lloyd. As I see it, two large cities might be destroyed, or darkness falls upon them. They grow silent. I feel somehow, I can prevent it, or at least try to prevent it from happening, but no one will believe that rather extraordinary story. They're not so crazy, of course, since I have a little trouble believing it myself. So, I have a dilemma. The story sounds bizarre, even to me, so that I do not see how I really can convince people of it. In addition, as Hurrian correctly stated, if we did run this or put it on the net, it could cause mass hysteria, which in itself will injure or kill a whole lot of people. But, if I am correct about the murky future, not doing anything might condemn people to disaster. I think the only rational direction is to try to convince people. But I must say, I do not know how to do that, and if we did, how would we prevent the hysteria that would follow. As you can see, Lloyd, I am indecisive. What to do? How do we prevent a tragedy without causing one? I know I might have to prevent the tragedy by convincing everyone of the rationale of a preposterous story. So, I just have to empty two large cities, or maybe not if enough people will believe in this fantastic story, which makes the whole thing absurd. Other than that, I would say, getting back to the sailing analogy, things are on an even keel."

"Abraham, you know, you talk funny!"

"You should see the way I think. No. I've got to see the good psychiatrist again to see if she can help straighten things out."

"So, you think that you're nuts?"

"Please, not so severe. I obviously have had a traumatic event happen either in my remote past or recently that I have generalized into a condition that has me running around two cities, trying to empty them of people, all so I will not face the true reality, which I am avoiding at all costs."

"I don't think I get it."

"I just said that I was nuts. The only thing is that there are things I cannot explain. There is a reality outside my head here. I upset electronic doors, I can memorize the dictionary or almost anything else that I really want to. I used to be fairly quick, but this is ridiculous. I have the magic touch. The touch that makes grown men raving God-fearing moonies. The smell, yes, my sense of smell is so heightened I have to sort of turn it off. Along with that I seem to have acquired some type of fondness for dogs. I want to run with a dog in the forest. That's all outside my head, although I guess the dogs are not. Inside I have memories that I shouldn't have. I remember the forest, from the top of the trees to the musky floor.

And, of course, I remember my other wife, Helen, despite the fact that I have never been married before. No, I'm not nuts, Lloyd. Some of the things I am experiencing are too real. They are not my thoughts, but the memories feel so real. And then of course there are the things I can actually do. No, I am not psychotic. The explanation is simple. I'm possessed!"

"You mean like a dybbuk?"

"Yeh, I guess so, maybe like an assembly of dybbuks. And not all the dybbuks are human. Not ghouls or some such thing, just not human. I seem to have so many memories that are not mine. Some may be extraterrestrial. Here we are at the Zephyr. Let's get our credits tapered and take off. Homeward bound."

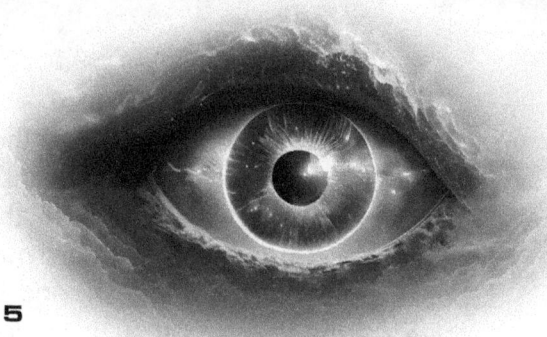

CHAPTER 15

Prescient Or Perverse

We approach the home of the Abbie. The Seri is standing outside the front door clearly distressed.

"Abbie, Abraham. I'm so relieved to see you. I had such a bad feeling about the trip. I was just sure you were going to be seriously hurt. I had an unshakable premonition myself. Thank God it was nonsense. Oh, hi, Lloyd. How are you."

"Fine, Sarah, but your husband here, seems a little mixed up."

"Abbie, Abraham, I've so much to tell you. It's definite. I'm pregnant. At my age and perimenopausal! I can't believe it after all these years. I've been taking the reps, but you know that's nothing new. They never found anything wrong with either of us, and I guess they were right. I still can't believe it, but it's real! Thank God!

What do you mean mixed up, Lloyd? Abbie, are you still hearing those voices?"

The Seri takes the Abbie's hand and signals to the Lloyd to enter the house.

"No, it's not voices, but it never was exactly voices. No, it's kind of like a fixed delusion. I don't hear or see anything unusual except I have this feeling of a visitor in my mind. I would dismiss all that and put myself on some type of mood drug except for the fact that if I touch people, and I will it, I can make them do things or believe certain stories. The other minor problem is that some of the stuff the transformed folks come out with. So, I have this strange effect on people, and I have this drive to depopulate cities. California cities in particular."

"Oh, I was hoping all that had cleared up. Abraham, how do we solve this and get you back to normal? You've got to see Naivir again."

"Oh, not to worry. I don't have to see anyone. You see, it's quite clear to me now, Sarah. I've been invaded by a foreign being, probably from outer space. If that's not probable, then I've just been possessed by demons, or dead spirits, or rather live spirits of dead people, dybbuks, you know, or . . ."

The Seri served some tea. At the Abbie's pronouncement, she knocks over the cup spilling the liquid on the floor.

"Abbie, don't even joke like that! You sound so like you are out of your mind!"

"Out of my mind is a clear and reasonable assumption, except I can't quite figure out how I do some of the things that I do and how I know some of the things I know. Quite the conundrum."

"Look, Abraham. You have to see Dr. Naivir again. You seemed to get along okay with her. Perhaps there is something she can help with, and it couldn't hurt. I need to know what's going on."

"Well, she certainly felt I was troubled, but at the time, I just wanted to prove I could do what I said I could. I will make another appointment. Maybe she knows of other cases like mine. I may have some sort of power of the mind, you know, the extrasensory stuff that you can unleash somehow or other. Nobody's ever been able to demonstrate it effectively, but perhaps I will be the first living documentation. If that's the case, then I could sit back and explore me rather than trying to convince whole cities to evacuate."

"Wait a minute! You're pregnant! Sarah, it's taken me a while to awaken to that fact. Oh, no, I just dropped my cup. This is wonderful. And I knew, I knew, dammit, I knew! That kinda throws a clinker into this all being in my head! Oh well, when, Sarah, when is it going to happen? What should we name our boy? My God, this is exciting!

"Seven months from now. I can't remember the exact date. I was so shocked. Yes, it is a boy! The doctor ran a check of the DNA makeup because of my age. It's perfect."

"Sarah, you're not so old, honey! Let's see. I forget. You can't be much more than ninety and having a baby!"

"Abraham, I'd kill people for saying far less. You know, Abbie, you've always been a little crazy. So, this personality and humor are quite normal, but this drive of yours, this desperation, is so unusual. I wish I could help.

Do you really feel that some dead spirit is in your mind? Do you really hear voices?"

"You mean like your voice, Sarah?"

"No, Abbie. You know what I mean."

"I don't hear any voices. As a matter of fact, I feel perfectly normal, but I have strange memories and knowledge, stuff that I've never experienced. Sometimes there is an image. Picture an image or a sense of vastness, unending stars and planets, limitless renewal of lives, marvelous beings stretched across time, folded and unfolded. There is no beginning, no end. There is a circular infinity, which I can't understand. But I understand that I'm hungry. What's for supper?"

"Abbie, you always do that! Just when you're pouring out your feelings, you cut it off with some joke! Abbie, oh Abbie."

"It's protective. Otherwise, I will drown in a sea of speculation and fear. It's therapeutic to come back to the here and now and look at the little ridiculous things in every situation. At the same time, I wish to do grand and glorious things like saving two cities and still want supper. Don't you think that's kind of absurd? Did Moshe stop for lunch when he parted the sea or climbed the mountain? Did anyone have to pee as they were walking across the Sea of Reeds? Did someone call for a bathroom break? How could they not?"

"Abbie, you're hopeless. I'll whip up something. Lloyd, you're invited, of course. Abbie, call Naivir."

"I've already done that. She doesn't have a regular time but she'll make time this evening at 1800 for another consultation, so we have just enough time to eat."

The Lloyd stares at the Abbie, and his brow is furrowed.

"Uncle, there is something different about you. You have a power and a presence now that wasn't there before. You know I've never been a religious man until very recently, that is, but I think you've been touched by the hand of God. You have been chosen for a new direction for our world. Think of how our forefathers, and the prophets and the judges, how they were all scorned in their day. Many were thought to be crazy."

"They probably were, judging by my own condition. I dunno, folks. I have a change in my capabilities, my memories, and my senses. I think I'm ready for a brain transplant or at least some engram rerouting.

Enough of this, let's sup. By the way, we should think of a name for the new sprout. Isaac has a nice ring. It seems to me that Abraham should have an Isaac, don't you? Anyhow Izzy almost rhymes with crazy, a chip off the old block. My great-grandfather's name was Isaac, and it would be nice to remember him. Let's see. How else can I make a strong case for that name?"

"Isaac, yuk! Oh, hell, let the baby be well, and you can call him anything you want, Abbie. Anyhow, I don't like talking about the child until he's born."

"Okay, maybe he'll be born in Winnipeg, so we should call him Winn or Winnie. And then, during his young years, he really will be Winnie the Pooh. On the other hand, I want to visit the Chicago area before we reach the promised plain. If he's born in the windy city, we could still call him Winn, or Wind, or Gas, or Chic."

"Abbie, you're off again and again and again. Why Winnipeg, why Chicago?"

"I'll tell you as long as you won't send me straight to the funny farm. When I let my mind relax for a second, memories seem to emerge. Why Chicago?

I'll tell you. There are some people there that are important to me. There is a wife —"

"A wife! What are you talking about? We have never been apart for long since we moved to North America, and you have never been to Chicago."

"Well, it was not me when we married. But I remember. Her name is Helen or Bette. There are two girls that I cannot see as well, and there is a boy, about 12 years old, Ike or Ian. I feel that I'm responsible for those people. I have deep feelings for the boy and the woman. I have a promise I made to the boy that I have to keep. Do you see the need for a brain transplant now?"

"Abraham! Are you telling me that you have another family? That's impossible!"

"Not in this body, I haven't. No, this is just a memory and not the only one I have. You know, I have worked on an assembly line and made hide-a-beds, and I have stalked a deer or maybe a moose and brought it down with my bare teeth. I'm even attracted to the nectar of flowers. You know when you're as crazy as I am. It's sooo broadening!"

The Seri and the Lloyd look at each other and appear to be quite concerned for the Abbie.

"Abraham, go see your psychiatrist! You scare me when you rant like this!"

"I'm sorry, Sarah, but I know these people exist just like I know the back of my hand. Hmm, now that's stupid."

"What's stupid, Abraham? Are you coming off this talking tangent?"

"No, the saying is stupid. I know that these people exist, but I actually don't know the back of my hands that well. I'm probably not bad on the back of my right, but not the back left. But I don't really know either that well. I have never really made a study of hands. Perhaps that expression comes from the time people used to read palms and lifelines and junk like that. I know my palm or the back of either hand less well than how to make key lime meringue pie, especially without the edges of the meringue shrinking."

"Abbie, has anybody ever told you sometimes it's hard to hold a serious conversation with you? Sometimes you are lovable and sometimes just exasperating."

"Sarah, I think the next line should be, 'get thyself to a psychiatrist Abraham, thus sayeth the Sarah.'"

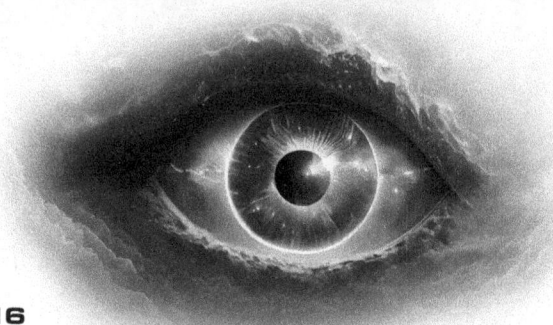

CHAPTER 16

Wacky Or Wondrous

The Abbie knocked on the Dr. Naivir door and was welcomed in. The doctor sits in a chair and motions for the Abbie to sit opposite her.

"Thank you for seeing me on such short notice, Doc."

"I'm happy to see you again, but if you are looking for ongoing care, and I suggest you consider that seriously, I cannot arrange that at this time. I'm seeing you because you called, and I suspected you needed some crisis intervention for the situation you are in at present. Let's talk about the present, and if you agree to the need for some ongoing care, I can suggest other people you could call."

"Well, Doc. I could remain in therapy forever. I've got so many character flaws there is enough grist to turn the mills infinitely. However, it's this fixed delusion about which I want your opinion."

"So, are you coming for my opinion this time and not your wife?"

"Yes, I will acknowledge that there is something very strange about me. In fact, more alien than the peculiar things that have always been there. I'm now the strangest of the strange, weirdest of the weird, super as the supernatural. I believe I can say this with all modesty."

"You have quite a sense of humor Abraham. I understand from you that you have a good trick with the dictionary."

"It is not a trick. It is not a delusion. It is just fact. I can memorize anything and very quickly."

"Perhaps we should get that out of the way right at the beginning. Are you familiar with this dictionary? I found this on my shelf and brought it out especially. Here, take a look at it. Is it similar to the one you have at home?"

"No, it's different than the one I looked at in my home, which matched the one in the library in the Chicago area, or Wescan or somewhere I have never been, not in reality but in my mind, of course."

"So, you cannot do the trick with this dictionary?"

"Oh, I'll be able to tell you the definition of any word, just not the page number, and the definition may not be in the precise language of that book. Boy, I would be overpowering in that old dictionary game."

"Give me the definition of septemvir."

"You don't have a lisp, do you, Doc? You're not trying to talk about the ninth month, are you?"

"Mr. Benterah, are you avoiding facing this issue with jokes, or are you here to face some things about yourself?"

"I'm here to try to find a foothold in reality, no jokes."

"Good, now tell me about that delusion. Is it something like the dictionary thing?"

"I didn't mean to leave you with the wrong impression. I have no delusion about the dictionary. It is one of the strange realities I'm battling with. Septemvir . . . it's a noun that refers to a group of seven men, especially in ancient Rome, associated in some office or work. A septemvirate is a government under septemvirs; hence, there is an office or rank of a septemvir. I have never used that word, so I'm just reading it from my mind dictionary."

The doctor raises her eyebrows and opens her mouth slightly.

"That's very impressive. Very impressive. You can do that with any word?"

"Yep, any word in English. I know Hebrew cause I have spoken it for years, but my command of the language is minuscule compared to English. That was not always the case."

"Hmm. Tell me about this delusion, Abraham."

"Well, do the doors of your building work, Doctor?"

"Yes, they do."

"Well, they don't for me. That's part of my delusion that I can physically bump into. This delusion can give me a bloody nose."

"So, you don't really believe that this is a delusion? You believe that the experience happens to you. If that's the case, then it's not a delusion. But something in you believes that you are possessed, or you wouldn't have come here."

"You're right. I don't think I'm cuckoo. I believe I'm possessed. I want you to tell me whether you believe this to be a syndrome that you have seen or are aware of through the psychiatric literature. Perhaps I am an acquired idiot-savant syndrome. I don't know if those have been described. I should read a psychiatric text; it shouldn't take me very long. I seem to have knowledge of things that I have never directly experienced. I have glimpses of vast stretches of space and time. I feel I know what the inside of a beehive looks like from the perspective of a bee. I know what it's like to run in a wolf pack, I think."

"Mr. Benterah, Abraham, how can you really think that you were in a beehive or ran with a wolf pack?"

"Well, try this on. I know what it is to live in Chicago, and there are people there that I know, even though

I have never set foot in the city. You probably won't believe this, but I phoned the number in my memory and asked for Helen Bette, and the woman answered in the affirmative. I asked if Ike Ian was there, and she said yes. I disconnected because it was too much for me. How did I know about those people? I have this fixed belief in my mind that L.A. and San Francisco are going to be destroyed in some catastrophic dark event. I would be truly happy to put these down as delusions, but I keep banging into these doors and getting a bloody nose. I can change people if I want to, just by touching them. By God, I was shot in the chest just a couple of days ago, and there is just barely a trace of a wound. It healed while I was unconscious, and when I awoke, I was tired, exhausted, but healed."

"Mr. Benterah, come down from your reverie. Please let us examine some reality here."

"Dr. Naivir, I know the date, the time, the place, the person. I am oriented, therefore, in the three spheres. Do a mental status on me, and I'll be there. I feel calm, and yet I can at will experience a flood of memories that I've never experienced. I can control the situation, both the horizontal and the vertical. I don't have to act on my feelings rather, it's that it seems to be the only rational thing to do."

"What seems the rational thing to do, Abraham?"

"Well, Dr. Naivir, here we go. I believe, rather I know, that the City of Angels and San Francisco are going to be destroyed in some fashion. A great darkness is going to descend. Life as we know it could disappear. I don't see exactly what happens, but I can detect nothing from the city after the disaster—no light or sound. I'm not sure what the disaster is going to be. It probably will be the Great Mother of all quakes. All the disaster predictions fostered by the newsmakers suggest that the southern part of California will be violently reclaimed by Nature, by fire, or by some power. Anyhow, something is going to happen unless, unless, unless I can bring out the truth, or change things, or bring forth some good people, thirteen, maybe less."

"What do you mean the truth Abraham?"

"I don't know. Maybe I am getting mixed up with my namesake in the Bible. Perhaps that's why I believe this whole thing can be prevented by the identification of some good people, at least a few, people who are not brain-dead religious fanatics but recognize the degradation of society. We must find individuals who are not after each other or fame or fortune or to prove their particular view of the world. I think that probably incorporates everyone. No one is for people anymore, or a just society, or fairness and balance. They are for issues, women, men, LGBTQIA+, heterosexuals, mothers, fathers, children, race, disabilities, undisabilities, and people against people who belong to the wrong group. We are split into tribal groups that live uneasily with each other.

This all sounds like a faintly familiar story, no? Sounds rather self-important also, no? This is one crazy idea, and I know that, but I do not feel absolutely brainless. A little fardrait, perhaps, but not insane."

"And what happens if you fail in your quest to identify the right type of people, Mr. Benterah? What happens to you?"

"If I fail to save the cities, then I must go with my people, my family, my friends, my relatives, my close contacts, and my world. We must wend our way to Winnipeg, the dying prairie town in Wescan. Winnipeg, the town, was the former breadbasket of what used to be Canada, west of Ontario and far from the two largest oceans. On the way to that frigid flat, I must stop in Chicago, or at least somewhere around that once-great city. It was a wonderful town once. There I must meet with my other family, Helen and Ian, and the girls. We must all wend our way to Winnipeg. I must teach Ian the skills to be self-sufficient so that he can make his own mark in the world. He will travel to the east, perhaps to the land of language disruption, and there he will develop a new nation and culture on the spoils of the old.

In Winnipeg, we will dwell and prosper among the inhabitants, including the mosquitoes. God, what am I talking about? I get in a run, and my brain takes over my mouth without me activating it. Anyway, I feel that the destruction of the promised land is to be undone in a new northern pact. On our trek, a young wolf will guide us on the way. Don't ask me why there is a wolf in my musings, but I feel I have spent some time as a wolf. In fact, this wolf may be my son. And that's not the nuttiest story I could tell you! If we need food, I can easily find and extract honey from the hives of bees. I can hear them in the air and smell them no matter where they happen to be. No problem. I haven't actually done this, but I know I can. I know the inside of a hive intimately. Now how's that leading your weird parade? What I just related is not just weird, it's bizarre, preposterous, loony, daft, demented, deranged, unhinged, distracted, dotty, and I might say rather unbalanced!"

"This is a lot to comprehend. What are you afraid of, Abraham? Is there something in your life that is falling apart that you must save? Is there something horrible that is emerging from your past that you're trying to suppress? Perhaps it is the vast destruction of the Middle East and what that did to your previous childhood home of Israel. I don't really believe in multiple personalities, and these other lives you imagine you have had are an attempt to suppress some greater fear, some greater reality that is trying to break through. You are afraid of that reality, and I think you are scrambling to keep those thoughts suppressed.

You are filling your mind with other experiences and people in order to aid the suppression.

Talk to me about your past, the Destruction. What do you remember of that horrible time?"

The Abbie gets up and paces the floor in front of the doctor and shakes his head.

"I've been here now for a long time and left Israel as a teenager. I remember the constant tension and threats. People had been living in those circumstances for over a hundred and fifty years. There were always discussions about further concessions and two parliaments to decide on the direction of that small piece of land. New models were developed that seemed one would never think of introducing or expecting except in the holy land, where miracles should happen. Miracles did not happen. At least, not 40 years ago. What happened was a devastating nuclear explosion and retaliation. Now there are hundreds of miles of uninhabitable land surrounding much of Israel, and many are a little more at risk of developing leukemia. Our family left before the cataclysm, quite by accident. My family always felt bitter. They were bitter against the rest of humanity for their inaction, for allowing this all to happen. When I think about it retrospectively, it is hard to know what else could have been done. Sometimes there is no right way.

But I was young, and I came to a new and exciting country. I have never felt great fear grinding in the pit of my stomach since that time. And now, although I seem to have something grinding in my head, I have no fear in my gastric mucosa. No, I have a peptic headache but a tranquil tummy."

"Joking is often a way to defend against fear, Abraham. Our time is just about up. If you wish, despite what I said at the outset, I will continue to see you and arrange an appointment with someone else in the future, so you can meet and see if the person is suitable. I can make a return appointment. I do think your thoughts have something to do with your past, but the demonstration of your knowledge of words is very interesting indeed."

The doctor stands and touches her pad, presumably to enter the appointment. She makes a gesture to the door, indicating the Abbie should leave.

"Yes, depending on the circumstances, I would like to keep meeting with you."

"Good. If that is the case, I have some homework I would like you to do in the next two weeks. I'm going on a holiday, but we will set a time when I get back. I want you to think of things that would make you feel more in command of yourself. I also want you to think of what you most fear happening to you, and we will decide how rational it really is."

"The homework I will try, and the time we can set up, but the location is another matter. If my prescience is correct, location, location, location will be all important. Are you going with your family, I hope?"

"That is none of your concern, Abraham. Let us set a date for two weeks today at 1600 hours here in my office. Then there will be no doubt of the location."

"It is out of concern that I hope you're going with the family, far away from here. I am not sure that L.A, and hence this location, will be here two weeks from today. If, on the other hand, L.A. is still communicating with us in more than a grunt or a call for help in a fortnight, then I certainly will seriously think of travelling back to be here as well. Yep, I guess if the city is still on the air in fourteen days, then it will be proof positive that I am truly disturbed and, furthermore, have no insight into my derailment. I, therefore, am or will be part of a fixed delusional system. I will then be really quite ready to do some good work on myself. Perhaps even those automatic doors you have on the building will work for me at that time."

"The doors are curious. Perhaps I will have you demonstrate that for me two weeks from today. Our time for today is now up."

"We'll meet again, don't know where, don't know when, but I know we'll meet again some sunny day . . . So long, Doc. See you in the funny papers."

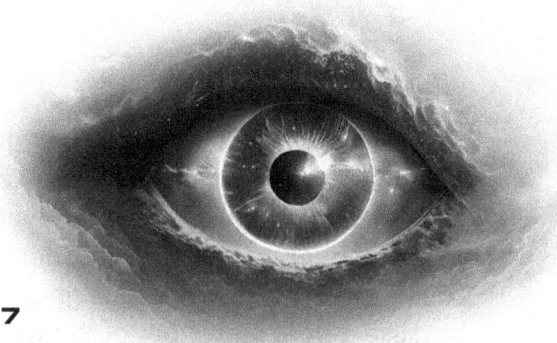

CHAPTER 17

The Prophecy

Through the window, we see the Seri sitting in the living room watching a screen. We hear her getting up as Abbie enters the home.

"Abbie, is that you? How did it go with the doctor? What did she say?"

"I think I convinced her."

"You convinced her of your prophecy and . . . and your prescience?"

"No, I think I convinced her that I'm mishuga. However, she's going on a vacation, and so are we, along with anyone we can convince to come with us."

"Look, Abbie. I really don't know what to do with you. A vacation I can go for. We both need it after all this business, and we need to reattach. But I thought you were going to speak to the newsmakers again, Abbie. You know, you are actually making me believe in the stuff, which I guess goes to show how much I actually have faith in you. I would like to leave on a lovely holiday, but if, on the other hand, you think that the area is going to be destroyed, I don't know what to do. We would have to warn people and save our neighbors, our friends. I just don't know how we could possibly convince the neighbors or our friends because it does sound out of this world crazy!

Don't you think it's worth a try to make the newsmakers understand? If they come out with something, at least it might make it possible for us to convince more people to leave."

The Abbie stands up, rubs his head, and sighs,

"Over two centuries ago, the reporters, or investigative reporters as they liked to be known, gradually stopped reporting the news and, with their cameras whirring, began making it. Even revolutions would stop to await the news coverage, which might help their cause. With the tremendous power of the digital message, they could and would take any situation and make it news. Like the scientist not being able to observe a subatomic experiment because the very act changes the observations, the news agencies changed the results by being there. They often were sincere, but that didn't matter. They lost perspective when they gained the power to inform, then reform, then form. They have lost the ability to report, and often they are unaware of that loss of ability. They research, but the research was limited to things that could be understood quickly and briefly. They probably just give their constituents what they want to hear, and by doing that, they shape control and direct public and private opinion. They are responsible to no one but their paymasters, and since the owners control private and pubic minds, they wield vast influence. Their news is not fake, as it once was famously called, but the power, as I said, is enormous."

"I think you mean public minds, Abbie."

"I sez what I means, and I means what I sez. In many ways, the very cornerstone of a free society depends on a free and independent media, but that media power has gradually become an extremely powerful force. If you don't have an open, free media, you have a controlled society, or at least one that can be manipulated. If you have a free media, by virtue of their own greed and pomposity, they present all opinions they feel as real news as reality to the society with the same judgmental or non-judgmental attitude. We are still having debates in the media about the theory of evolution and whatever the latest crazy creationist theory is presented as equal arguments. One is a proven fact; we can see bacteria evolve constantly, so these should not be presented as equal and valued opinions. That is only one of scores of examples. When the media continues to exploit the news, it actually stifles progress. It does not help society move forward. It is not that differing opinions should not be aired, but there should be some basis in fact to air those sides.

There is an irony here in the fact that the only entity that might be used to save this local society cannot be used because it might create havoc for some, and others will not believe it because of the track record. On the way home, I actually tried to get into one of the local offices. The only way I could manage it is by using the magic touch. Somehow, that's wrong, and it would not work for the masses. It's too individual.

Wait, are those dogs barking? God, it's like I want to go play with them."

The Abbie shakes his head and holds it. He is very troubled. Can we do something different?

"Forget the dogs, Seri. I did not know what to do. Individual people will bend to my will, but it's like playing newsmaker with that power. No, I think we had better reverse a remarkable and venerable trend and emigrate out of California. Let's start packing, and don't forget all the kids and the goats."

The Seri is now standing and pacing, holding her hands to her head.

"Oh, Abbie, what do you mean kids and goats and dogs? You scare me with that type of talk. I'm trying to believe in you, but you make it so difficult.

"There must be a way to convince people. We have such massive communication networks now, yet nobody believes in the communications. We have overdosed on our ability to correspond. Maybe what you're saying, Abbie, is that we need an overall morality and someone who can make it stick. We need a God. No one else will do."

Is that what you mean by the kids and goats, our flock? Are we to return to the days of wandering tribes? Is that what you really envision?"

"It's just a biblical expression. I want all our friends and relatives to come with us on our quest. I'm going to contact all our relatives. First, I'll view Lloyd and make sure he and his insufferable wife, and family, take this journey with us. Let's make haste. There's not a lot of time, even in a relative fashion. If I'm wrong, we've gone on a very expensive vacation for no good reason. If I'm right, we have at least saved those people who are near and dear to us."

You might be right, Seri. Perhaps it would be better if we were able to return to an old way of life, a rebirth of a past world, with a just omnipotent God. It will be a shot at resetting history. We should turn the clocks back and start them ticking again. Hmm, I guess clocks haven't actually really ticked for over two hundred years, and almost no one uses a clock or a watch. I am not sure where that came from. If we did manage to redo history and turn back time, how long will it tick forward before the battery needs recharging again? It might not even reach midnight or morning. But some of us will have a chance. Perhaps we will change a part of the world again, just like in those olden, not-so-golden days. That's what we're doing, I think."

"You think. Horrible destruction, Abbie; it's all so unfair to all those people. We can't just go off and leave them. There must be some way to warn them. If what you see is true, so many lives are at stake. If you really believe this, there must be a way to do this within our present system. Can we possibly help anyone by becoming a wandering tribe again, carrying a message that people will hear long before we arrive and analyze several times over? We have to think of a way to do this, Abbie, in the context of the here and now. We communicated and touched people in the past through war and wandering. You can't make me believe that's the best way to do all this now if there is any sense or morality left in this world!"

"Que Sera, Sarah. We will spread the story as far and as wide as we can. Perhaps it will have an effect as we leave the city with our entourage. I just don't know how to reach the people. What should I say? Hi there, folks. I have a message from God, or from my mind, or from a space invader. Actually, it's probably better if I tell everyone that there is a little person or little something in my mind that's telling me to do this. That ought to make them believe in me! There is something so pure about being completely mishuga. I could show them some of my newfound abilities, which are kind of miraculous, but there is too much cynicism today to make people believe. Even miracles will look like some type of computerized image. I feel we are all paralyzed. We can no longer distinguish between right and wrong. There is no clear good and bad, perhaps there never was, but we can no longer distinguish between the important shades of gray. We have failed to be able to draw any line in the sand anywhere along the spectrum of human activity. Therefore, we cannot learn from one another, no matter what. You know, as I think of it, it is the loss of belief in science, which is the knowledge of reality. It was considered wonderful that there was something mystical in science, chaos theory. Therefore, one could drop that whole concept of proof and depend on one's own intuitive knowledge. And since we cannot and will not learn, it has heralded the onset of the Age of Stagnation and Me think. Yes, the Age of S and M, following the Age of Aquarius.

I can't think of anything else that we can do other than the chance to replay history. Something has to happen to reset time and start it counting down or up again. The future will unfold thusly, Sarah. You will bear the son that will begin the trek to a new cradle of our own civilization. You will bear the new kernel, and you and your son will be an integral part of that fountainhead. *Your* seed will be the words of your story, and your deeds will spread over the planet as they did in the past. It is as it will be."

"Abbie, suddenly, you didn't sound like yourself again. You lapsed into that strange formal sounding speech for a moment. At times you sound almost rational, at least as rational as you usually sound, and then you adopt slightly different mannerisms and voice. You start sniffing and snorting! What's happening to you, Abbie? What is happening to us? Are you feeling all right? Oh, I wish you'd stop with all this talk. I want my Abbie back again. I don't know whether to believe you and accept all this or to call Dr. Naivir and have you committed."

Merge.

This host can operate independently, and too much interference is causing a problem with Sarah and Lloyd. It is difficult to balance what needs to be done and keeping this host safe. This is a difficult task. But this host must not die as the others have. That has almost happened already, but repair was possible. The host must be left to act in his normal fashion. Submerge.

"I'm okay, Seri. Okay, I think. I don't know exactly what's happening to me. I felt like I just blacked out for fifteen seconds. Sarah, I don't know what will happen, but the urge is so powerful that I have to play out the string and see this thing through. My whole being is telling me that this is right. I've got to see this to the end, no matter what. Please hang in there with me, honey."

"What did you mean by all the kernel and seed stuff, Abbie? What do you mean a new path for our civilization?"

The Seri is holding the Abbie's face between her hands and looking at him; tears are streaming down her face.

"I don't remember saying anything about that, Sarah. But I know what it means. It's the personal path of civilization for us on this planet. Seeds are seeds of the mind. If we can plant them in enough people, they will grow. If they thrive, they will reform a wider civilization. We, if we are lucky and have the courage to see it through, will return to a better and more gentle and caring society.

But now we must act to save as many people as possible from what I think is going to be some type of disaster. I will reach out to all we know. Lloyd has left, but I will contact him to convince his family. It will take something to move his wife out of the Golden Gate city. It will take more to try to coax out any of those strange daughters of his. But we've got to try."

The Abbie taps something on his wrist and starts speaking into it.

"Lo, Lloyd, Uncle Ab here, as you can see. I trust you are ready to take to the highways and the byways and travel to a magnificent land. Is the family ready to go on this adventure to the land of milk and honey, cheese and wheat?"

"I want to follow you, Abbie, but the wife and children seem less ready to wend with me."

"Lloyd, it's time to use some persuasive charm, boyish humor, wit, courage, advice, dominance, intelligence, art of the spoken word. Debate, flourish, do it, Lloyd. I know you can!"

"I dunno, Abbie. I don't think Gloria will do it for me, and I know she won't for you."

"Lloyd, sometimes you just bring me down to earth after I begin believing in my persuasiveness. Hmm, I don't have the time to slip down there and touch her heart. I want to be able to leave as soon as possible. In the next day or two, we hopefully will hit the road."

"Well, maybe I can convince her to go to Sacramento for a few days, and then maybe we can do something when we are there. I may be able to get a couple of the girls, but not all of them with their families."

"Sacramento, Lloyd? We're talking here about the Great Wend on our way to Winnipeg, not a sashay to Sacramento. Hey, I kinda like the alliteration; way to Winnipeg. Maybe, Pursue the Peg. Use alliteration, use force, use your wits, man!"

"I don't think Gloria is going to buy into this, Abbie."

"Okay. We'll use another type of charm, Lloyd. But we've got to get moving quickly. I will send you a document in a few minutes, witnessed by my wife, entitling you to a twenty-five percent share of my wealth for you and your family if you leave tomorrow afternoon or when I ask you to so we can rendezvous in Sacramento.

The Seri spring up with her mouth wide open, and there is anger on her face. The Abbie holds up his hand.

"Lloyd, I will meet you in Sacramento at 1800. It should only take me a couple of hours on the shooter at that time of day. Take arms since there is always the possibility of banditos. From there, we will immediately head to Reno, and then the next day, a late lunch in Salt Lake."

"Abraham Benterah, you've really done it this time! Promising your wealth, our wealth, to that worthless, good-for-nothing nephew of yours, and Gloria, that, that . . . How can you do that without discussing this with me? That's not your money; it's our money! Abbie, you cannot assume I will always go along with what you want. And this is something I don't want. If things are going to be rough, if I truly have a child, we can't squander our hard-earned credits on that no good . . ."

"Just one second, Lloyd, a rear attack. Seri, have I ever let you down? I know I didn't discuss this with you, but there's no time. I know the money belongs to both of us, but I'll make up whatever I lose, and I vow that both of you, you and our unborn son, will be looked after. It's important I do this. Trust in me, despite the fact that I'm mad, mad, I say."

"Abraham, I believe in you, but this you have to admit, this is stretching reality, even for you. How can we lose all those credits to people that have shown that they are unreliable?"

"I admit that, Sarah. This is ten out of ten on anyone's scale of unreality. My whole being says that there will be a calamity in the San Fran, L. A. area. I can't leave them behind, no matter what. They are family, and I promised Nate I would look after Lloyd. I know this is pouring everything into some absurd vision, but we have to move with the adventure. I also think Lloyd is a little more stable now."

"Abbie, I'll go with you anywhere. I don't know why I do, but when it comes down to it, it's a faith in you."

The Seri stands and takes Abbie's face in her hands and puts her lips to his. This is called a kiss. It is experienced as a pleasant sensation by the Abbie.

"I love you, my woman. Thank you."

"Lloyd, are you still there?"

"Abbie, Gloria says she wants a third and for you to send it before we leave. If that is done, she and two of the girls say they will go with you but only to Salt Lake. At that point, they are going to turn around and go back to San Francisco, as long as nothing has happened, of course. She wishes to know now when the transfer of money will happen?"

"Lloyd, how did you wind up with such a sweet wife? The milk of human kindness flows in her veins. Let me get this straight. Goria, or rather Gloria, wants a third of my assets to travel to Salt Lake City and then return to Frisco. What kind of nonsense is this anyway? Allow me to speak to the dear girl.

Hello, Gloria, my love. I wish to save the lives of you and your family, and I'm willing to sweeten the pot a bit, but this is ridiculous. Not that I wish to upset you, Gloria, but I spoke to a Magiman in the Frisco the other day, and he assured me an ill wind was a blowing toward Frisco Bay. Did Lloyd not tell you of the magical feats I have been performing? I believe I even saved your husband's life with one of them. Think of these things, my dear, and see how much you want to gamble on being wrong."

"You pimp, you may be able to twist Lloyd's head around, but you can't con me. If you want me to leave now, you'll have to pay sweetly. I don't know what the con is, Abbie, but if it's important enough to bribe for, I'm in the driver's seat. Now, stuff that up your ass."

The Gloria's voice is very high-pitched and harsh. It is not melodic like the Seri's.

"I really don't do that sort of thing, niece-in-law. Let me put it to you another way. I have, as you well know, some influence in political matters, at least where bribes can be influential. Therefore, that takes care of most matters. I have supported Lloyd on many occasions, which might have been difficult for both of you had I not.

Now, I want you to listen very carefully, which is something quite difficult for you. I hereby vow, in the presence of God, that I will banish you. You will be left with nothing unless you go along with this. I am also withdrawing my previous offer completely. I am leaving California and will not return. You will never hear from me again if you remain behind. Now you can put that wherever it gives you the least pleasure!"

"You would never abandon, Lloyd!"

"Here this! I am leaving, and everything I own is migrating with me. I'm going to settle in another country that still has some semblance of a government—Canada West. I assure you, nothing will be left for Lloyd and especially not for you. My generosity has come to an end, and any oath I made to Lloyd's father has been fulfilled. Either journey to the junction of the Red and Assiniboine Rivers or your support ticket shrivels to nothing. If you are not going to be led, then you will not be fed and probably will be dead. Is that clear enough for you, Glorious?"

"You and your poetry are goddamn awful."

"My soul is the perfection of poetry, but my mouth perfidious. The decision is yours. We will not wait or lacrimate for you."

"Thirty-three percent, and I'll decide . . ."

"I will give you five, and I'll decide when and where you'll meet me. This is the complete piece, goodbye, niece."

The Abbie taps his wrist several times. This apparently breaks the connection to the Gloria.

"Let's go, Seri. Did I tell you we have to pass through Chicago? They say it's a wonderful town. Chicago, Chicago that wonderful town, Chicago, Chicago, I don't seem to know the words."

"Oh, yes, for the wife you have never met and a son and daughters. It is bizarre."

"I am not sure it is actually Chicago, but around there. I will know where to go when I get there. Besides it being a wonderful town, I owe Helen and Ian something, although I can't quite explain it. I just don't feel like leaving them out on that dessert alone. Also, perhaps I will learn the words to that song, Chicago, Chicago, that wonderful town, Chi."

"Abbie, stop! I hoped I was hearing things. I just don't get it! Abraham, who is this Helen—"

"She prefers Bette."

"BETTE then! Is this someone you knew before me or during our relationship? I have a right to know.

And I am also telling you that I have not bargained for the open marriage concept. I don't like the idea. I don't agree with it, and I don't care if others are doing it. Got it!"

The Seri is excited and raises her voice, stamps her foot on the floor, and clenches her fists.

"I don't believe in those things, either. And I don't know these folks, at least not in my present form. I, Abbie Benterah, have never, never known Helen or Ian Ike. But, as sure as I am standing here, I do know them very well and love them. I owe them something. They are connected, and I have spent considerable time with them. Much of it was not all that good for them, but I managed to make it up to them more recently. This has all got to do with all the strange stuff that's happening."

"What do you MEAN you spent time with them? You're talking in riddles again, Abbie. Are you talking about amnesia or something? You think there are some people that you have had something to do with but don't remember. I have known you since you were young. You have never been away that long from me. Not years, not even months. What on earth are you thinking?"

"I'm talking about the fact that I'm beginning to integrate my mind. I am beginning to integrate with . . . with my other self or selves, with the other memories. They have become clearer. Something has ensconced itself in my mind. There is a presence I can feel, and with it are these memories of places, animals, sights, sounds, smells, people, Helen.

On the one hand, I want to rid myself of all these thoughts which are not me. They're intrusive, and they're pushing me to do something about which I know nothing. And on the other hand, the feeling, the existence in my thoughts, gives me a breadth of knowledge, a sense of energy and vitality I have never imagined. I now have a sense of purpose and don't wish to surrender it, no matter how foreign it feels. The experience, at times, is overwhelming. If I allow myself the indulgence, I can wander into new worlds. There is a magnificent mist undulating out there in space. There is black matter composed of an aggregate of antiparticles swimming in nothingness and, on the other side of nothingness, somethingness. That's a word you will not find in any dictionary. Somehow, we are being touched; our world is being caressed. And within the vapor are worlds upon worlds, existence upon existences, patterns upon patterns. It's endless. Our world is readjusting, and some of it may disassemble. We must adapt to this revolution, and we must renew. If we fail to react, we may literally rupture, and I'm hungry. What's for supper?"

"Supper? What's for supper? Abbie, what are you talking about? You just rambled on about worlds and minds, you just started opening up to me, and then you closed up.

And make some type of joke. Relax? I've got to understand what's going on with you. Keep talking and tell me more of your thoughts. Don't worry, I can take it. I know you. I don't know what is happening, but I have confidence in you and in your mind. Just take some deep breaths and unload. It's so good to hear what is going on with you. For me, this is important, Abbie. Don't close down."

"When I relax and open my mind to the world within, its enormity demands closure. I feel I could lose myself in the vapor. I only peak at the thoughts, I only peer obliquely at those images, and then I must look away to avoid being consumed. They are too much to integrate at any one time. It's like being blind for a time before your vision is restored. The light can only be taken very gradually. I try to bring a little forward, digest and order it before going back for more. I'll keep you updated on the latest on the reverie of my inner mind, I guess, of my inner mind. I am not even sure whether these thoughts are all mine or someone else's. It is a little schizoid, Sarah. I experience the sensation of being split. That's why I went to see Naivir. On the other hand, I cannot ignore the overwhelming drive which says you must do what you must do. It is not truly a compulsion, but an enormously strong passion, that this is the right thing to do. I am praying to I am not sure who, that I am not acting recklessly, and that there is true purpose. I so hope that I will be justified in my actions since I am uprooting everything we have known. If I'm deranged or off the beam about my predictions, I'll be more than embarrassed. I will be mortified. Then, I'll have to speak to Naivir in earnest, if I can speak at all. If I'm even partly correct, in another 48 to 72 hours San Francisco and L.A. will be rubble, swallowed by fire, flood or a quake, with millions of lives lost. I cannot tell what happens because a great darkness descends, and I cannot pierce it. We will then be on the road that has not before been travelled. The road will lead to a cold northern dying community. That community will again begin to flourish. The road will not end there, for no road truly ends. One can reverse the direction, and the path can be trod on in many ways. Farther into the future, I see our descendants heading west, perhaps to Victoria on the coast. That, however, is well into the future."

"I guess time will reveal all of this to us, Abbie."

"Time will not tell. It may be a relative but knows nothing. The people who experience it will tell all. Now that's about as serious as I can get at one sitting. We must call all our loved ones and those acquaintances who have some trust in us, we must pack, and most importantly, we have to have supper. Shall we have supper first, Seri?"

CHAPTER 18

It's Safer In Sacramento

Merge. Not many are following Abraham Benterah. Should we have intervened in order to try to save more, or was it destined to happen? These are impossible decisions. They are now travelling in a vehicle called a shooter which receives its energy from the electrified road. Apparently, these are used for longer voyages, but only if the appropriate roads are available. There appear to be safety features built into the shooter.

Submerge.

"Abbie, Abbie, are you awake? You are the pilot, for God's sake!

"Sorry, Seri. I am here.'

"Abbie, do you have to drive so fast? Where's the fire? No, don't answer that. I know it will be behind us. Just slow down! You can't save the world or humanity if you become just another statistic on the shooter. Even the shooter is not foolproof, you know. Rare and unusual accidents caused by humans have happened."

"Sarah, you're the navigator; I'm the pilot. Anyhow, who said anything about saving the world? I want to save us and the family. No one else will listen except the few people I've touched. It just seems so inevitable, like there is no chance to save anyone else."

"What do you mean you're not saving the world? You've been talking about humanity, prophecy, evil, paths, and God speaking to you and showing you the future or am I the one who's having the hallucinations!"

"Remember, if there really are visions, I'm not hallucinating. I didn't say anything about God. I've thought of God as quite different, you know, big fellow, booming voice, grand visions. He has a pact with nature to allow the overthrow of the order of science and physics so that miracles may manifest. That would be God. This is different. This is plain stupid. Why would God reveal himself to me inside a beehive? What is happening to me seems to be some being that is flying by the seat of his pants! I do not know if the thing, the presence is male or wears pants. It almost seems as if he was looking for the right host, although he had no preconceived knowledge of whom or what that might be."

"Well, Abraham, what else could all this mean, other than the fact that I'm following a madman, whom I happen to be in love with, to meet another woman in Chicago, although that may not be the place, and then onto this place called Winnipeg. I think I will go back to the dybbuk scenario."

"Seri, it sounds like you've been listening to me . . ."

"Abbie, don't look at me when you speak; keep your eye on the line!'

"Seri, we'd automatically break if there was anyone in front, and it takes a couple of moves to detach. Our shooter is firmly hitched to the line. Anyway, you're the navigator, and I'm the pilot, so you have to tell me if I change direction and not comment on the progress. Now, where was I?"

"You were saying that we are not following the will of God, but perhaps a spirit, a dybbuk."

"No, you brought up the trickster, spirit, dybbuk idea. It's not a bad idea, but there are no spirits, dybbuks, devils, etc. No, this is something else. I guess the God idea or a little green man from somewhere else are possibilities not out of the question."

"So, you would rather believe that you've been taken over by an intelligence from outer space? That is not very comforting, Abraham. I'd rather this be a commandment from God. Anyway, why would a little green man want you to go to Winnipeg?"

"Why would anyone want us to go to Winnipeg? Have you heard how cold it gets in the winter up there?"

"No, how cold does it get in the winter?"

"It gets sooo cold that polar bears wear fur coats."

"Oy."

"Okay. There are six months of winter and six months of street repairs. Maybe Satan wants us to go there to freeze our collective asses off. No, that can't be right; he likes heat, not cold."

"Abbie, you just keep going in circles."

"Is that a navigation report or a statement about my lack of cerebration?

The Seri is looking out the window at passing malls, trees, and all the attributes of a place that has been her home for many years. A tear rolled down her cheek."

"It's definitely about your cerebration Abbie. It's the unusual state of your lateral mind. Abbie, it is sad to be really leaving,"

"I know, Seri, but it may not be pleasant around here in a short while. Let's talk about the Peg. It's not seventh heaven up there, but it might be the Promised Land for us. Because of global warming, the weather, although severe, will be tolerable. It has the potential to regenerate its flowing grain fields, rivers, lakes, and streams. It has prairie power, a distant horizon, and mosquitoes. It may be a sign from God or someone that knows something we don't. If the green men are from Mars, and we know they are not because we have been there . . .

Oops, it looks like we're nearing Sacramento. I think I spot that bridge in the distance. I told Lloyd that we would go through and meet him in North Highlands. It will be easier to make contact there. We will disengage from the shooter in a few minutes and meet at the abandoned shopping center."

"I can't wait to see Lloyd's wonderful family. I am being facetious about that. There's the center, and I do believe I see them by the side of the old grocery store. They actually came and even were on time! Gloria must have believed your threat!"

"Helloo, family! Are you ready to begin the big adventure?"

The Abbie and the Seri approach a group of people, one of which is Lloyd. The Gloria person appears to be shorter than average. Her hair is a very bright red, and all her clothes are bright red. There is nothing specific about her facial features, but she is scowling.

"I'm ready to do nothing of the sort, Abbie. Now what is this all about? Lloyd is telling me about visions of God, destruction of San Francisco, and who knows what all. You were always crazy, Abbie, but this time you really outdid yourself."

"Hi, Gloria. It's always a pleasure and a distinct privilege to see your kind face again. It was hard to pick you out in that getup. Hope all is well with you and your family."

"I'm going to puke, Abbie. Cut out the shit and tell me why the hell we are here!"

"Look, Gloria. Few things would give me a greater, albeit momentary, internal personal sense of sweet justification and revenge than to see you vomit or have marked discomfort, but there is time for pleasures like that later. Right now, there are more important things to concern us, than your self-centered world. We may well be witnesses from afar to the destruction of millions of people. I wish there were some way to convince people of the palpable danger that is soon to strike. I wonder if it's not too late. Perhaps there is some type of broadcasting station here that I can commandeer. Then I could at least broadcast the message. Perhaps I'll save some that way."

"It will cause mass hysteria if people really believe you, you idiot. You've already created the hysteria in my family. There are idiots in those cities, like my husband, Lloyd, who just might believe you. They'll probably saturate the shooter, somewhere a circuit will blow, and the catastrophe you predicted will happen on the shooter! That's your idea, isn't it? To become a prophet by creating your own calamity! What a shit you are, Abraham."

"Gloria! Don't speak to Uncle Abraham that way. He has seen the way and I believe in him. He has done many things, which are unexplainable, and he saved my life again. He must have been touched by the hand of God."

"Lloyd, the only supernatural thing going on here is the way this man can rot your mind. We had a great business going for us in the Frisco, and you let him talk you out of it. Moral issues, idiots, you're all idiots. I don't know why I stick with you."

"Now Gloria . . ."

The Abbie is upset and wishes to calm the Lloyd and Gloria.

"Children, children! Please let us not spat. In this case, Lloyd, a rare thing has happened. A true miracle!"

"What's that?"

"I think Gloria may actually have a point. That's the miracle. How can we get people out of the two cities without causing mass hysteria, power shutdowns, and calamity on the shooter because a googolplex of people invade it? Power outage itself could cause looting, fear, and hysteria. I certainly could create my own little catastrophe. Would I save enough lives considering the possible destruction? How many more lives would be lost because of my announcement? Would I save enough to make up for the carnage on the outways of the two cities? How many more do I have to save to make up for the mayhem, one hundred more, ten more, two more? If this is a divine inspiration, would somehow the people exit safely? Okay, presence! I need guidance here! A burning bush won't do! I need concrete answers. What do I do? I feel psychotic!"

Abbie is upset and pacing. The Seri comes up to him and puts her arm on his shoulder.

"Abbie, Abbie, are you okay? You went into one of your stuttering spells."

"I'm fine, Seri, other than I have a giant attack of ambivalence on how to proceed."

"Now, you're unsure of your prescience? This is not a good time to tell me after we have dragged Gloria and Lloyd here, and you've promised them the world."

"It's not so much that the feeling of impending cataclysm has gone, but the confidence that I had that somehow, I could in some way save the people is evaporating. Gloria's right. If I managed to broadcast my message, which I might be able to do to five or ten, with my touching power, I might cause mayhem. It would get around, and there would be a mass evacuation. Not enough people have airways, and the shooters would probably explode, even if a relatively small proportion of the population believed, or at least reacted to me."

"If they believe in you, perhaps you can instruct them in the importance of an orderly departure."

"When panic sets in, unfortunately, no one will wait for his neighbor."

"Tell them not to take their shooters at all. Tell them to walk or something."

"To walk, to walk, hmmm, to use their legs, would they have the time? Would the destruction wait? You know, if they bought the story of the destruction, they might believe in an orderly message of departure. Perhaps only the temporarily infirm and the very young would be allowed to take the shooter as a commandment of God. It might work."

"Surely, Abraham, a little white lie, twisting the law would be allowable to help with safe departure."

"According to a responsa by Meir ben Baruch of Rothenburg, a minor procedural rule of the court does not render the decision of the court nugatory. I take the reasoning that even if I were not specifically commanded thus, it would not be impolite to suggest such a possibility. I guess this is especially true since I don't know who, what, or if anyone is commanding me to do anything. Therefore, it would seem perfectly reasonable to save all the people I can, whatever way

I can, in the safest method possible. Now, since no one will be saved if I don't act, and I'm sure of the consequences, then I must act. I may have to touch my way into a Newsmaker station and make a little broadcast. This really shouldn't take long. I'd like you all to wait here, and I'll be back shortly."

The Abbie is leaving the group. He is running toward the shooter, made somewhat difficult because he is wearing heavy non-compliant blue pants, which we believe are called jeans.

"Uncle Abe, wait, I'll come with you. Perhaps I'll be able to help out."

"Thanks, Lloyd, but this will be a piece of cake and I would like you to stay here with the families and keep everyone happy. I can assure you that I will not be long because my most important goal is to put even more distance between us and frilly Frisco."

"Just a damn minute, Abraham! Do you really expect me, Gloria, to stand around here waiting for you?! I am not a nobody. If we stay here, we'll probably be blamed for your attempted newsmaker station break-in. You're likely to fumble it anyway. I am not going to stand for any more of this. We're going back. I cannot wait to feel and smell the streets of San Francisco again."

The Abbie stops and walks back to the group.

"Look, everyone, gather round. Listen to me, please! I admit to quirks in the past. However, you all have to admit that despite this family's trials and tribulations in the past, I have cared for the family. Generally, we have prospered. I have never agreed with the lifestyle of your family, Lloyd, which is abnormal according to my internal personal moral code, and although I disapprove of the preferences you and your family sometimes display, I have always helped and supported you. I have provided for all of you and protected you as best as possible. I did this even when lying or practicing some other type of deception was necessary. Never have I asked you to believe in me unfailingly; that is, up till now. I now ask you to believe in me for another day or two. Then if nothing happens, we will head back to our respective cities. You all will have the last laugh and at my expense.

"Lloyd, I'm going back. Your crazy uncle is going to get us all arrested or at least embarrassed. There's nothing for us out here and following this idiot will kill us all. If you're coming, come because me and the girls, at least, won't wait!"

"Gloria, please. I beseech you, for the good of the girls at least, don't go back, don't even look back, at least until I return from the newsmakers."

"Uncle, I have faith in you, and we will wait for you until you return."

"Lloyd, you'd have faith in a stone. You're off your rocker with this faith stuff, as is your nutty uncle. The girls and me are leaving!

"Don't worry, Uncle. I'll take care of my family. We will stay. We'll wait for you. God guide your way and bring and bring you back speedily to us."

It is clear that the Abbie is troubled with the arguments occurring. He is afraid to leave but wishes to try to convince more people to leave. They are standing outside in the sun. We can feel the intensity of the heat on the skin of the Abbie.

"Lloyd, thank you for your faith in me, even if I caused it. You're a little sickening but nice, nonetheless. Don't let them return, please! Seri, see if you can work some of your magic with them. I know my nephew and his formidable wife. Despite his intentions, I don't think Lloyd can follow through. Also, be careful; if it goes too smoothly, if the spell checker comes up with no mistakes, there's an error in the program."

"Go ahead, Abraham. I'll see what I can do here. If you feel that's the right way to go, as usual, I will support you with blind faith. I don't exactly know what's going on, but I do believe in you. Gloria and some of her kids, especially Tannis, still may leave, but perhaps I can prevail on her not to. As a family member, perhaps she will listen. I know her and how she thinks. She is not a stranger to me. Stranger things are happening now but not with her. What a funny thing to say to you! I think I just made one of your jokes."

"Wish me luck, doll. Why do you suppose it's so hard to save people? Is it possible that I am not supposed to save those people? And if not, why not? And who doesn't want the saving to occur? God? Intelligence from a distant planet? Okay, brain, what's going on? I know you're in there, my visitor. What do you want from me? Why are you forcing me to do all this? Are you forcing me to do all this, or are you just influencing me, opening up the window to the future? Is it real, or are you just screwing up the old pathways, giving me hallucinations so you can have some fun? Ding, ding, ding, here comes my wagon to take me to the funny factory. *Ding, ding, ding*, here comes my wagon, can't you hear the driver calling me *ee ee ee*? Just like the nuts that fall, I'm a little cracked that's all, *ding, ding, ding*, here comes my wagon, my kiddy car, my twuck! God help me, for I am strange and about to get stranger still. On to the newsmakers and damn the torpedoes. What the hell were torpedoes, anyhow?"

The Abbie is again upset. He interrogates his inner mind, trying to discover us. He taps his head as the group looks on with concern.

CHAPTER 19

Again, The Newsmakers

The Abbie enters a building with a sign that reads Zinger Communication Network. There is a at the reception desk with the name Susan Rosa. She is slightly darker skinned than the Abbie and has long black hair.

"How do you do, Ms. Rosa. Are you aware that your automatic doors are not functioning properly? No matter. Don't apologize. Just show me to the Zinger studio.

"You're . . . ?"

"Benterah, Abraham Benterah, young woman. Let me shake your hand and influence you in the story of the Almighty . . ."

"You cannot go in . . . why, of course, you can. It's on the third floor. Turn to your left after you leave the elevator. Who are you, Mr. Benterah? What message do you have for us.!"

"I'll broadcast it on the Interact."

"The Interact is operating right now, but for the message that you have to tell us of the return, I'm sure they'll let you interrupt the broadcast. Amber Pick is on the waves right now."

"If you have a point to pick, pick it with Pick. Touch 2389 8484 and let Amber shed a little light on your Picked point."

"You don't have that quite right, Mr. Benterah. It really goes . . ."

"That's okay. You can spare me. I must have heard that before being possessed. Otherwise, it should have been exactly correct. I never thought it was in the least catchy. Thank you so much, Susan, if I may call you that. By the way, I would suggest an immediate vacation, in an easterly direction. We are wending our way to Winnipeg, and you are welcome to accompany us. Whatever you decide, it is of the utmost importance that you take your leave of this place immediately, at least for a while. If you do take your leave, remind me to speak to your superior to ensure that they'll allow you to go immediately. Now, you said the third floor? Good, thank you again, and remember you are welcome to join us."

The Rosa person now has a look of tranquility but appears to be earnest.

"May the holy spirit be with you."

"That's interesting. The holy spirit hasn't been with me before, but there's no reason he shouldn't come along for the ride. There's no question that the force is with me, to quote the venerable classic series and all the rest of them. Well, my force, my brain companion, come out, come out wherever you are. Here we are on the third floor, my companion. Here's to show business and, above all, *L'chaim* to life."

The Abbie leaves the elevator machine and sees a man with a sign on his chest that says, Ralph. Ralph sees the Abbie as leaves the elevator and is angry.

"Hey, who the hell are you? Who gave you permission to be up here? Get the fuck out of here, or we'll have you thrown . . ."

The Abbie puts up his hand and, in doing so, touches the Ralph person.

"The name is Benterah, Abraham Benterah. I'm here to zing a little zong on the Interact tonight. Would you like to zing a little zong with me? You know, tonight won't be just any night. In truth, there may be no morning star for the west coast people. Thus, I want to zing into San Francisco and L.A. homes for a little parlay about the mother of all quakes. Perhaps it won't be a quake. That just seems like the most natural thing around here. Hasn't been a major one since 93, or 94, something like that. Anyhow, I suggest you take an immediate vacation my good man, because

I don't believe Sacramento may be far enough from the epicenter to be free of the rumble of the rubble, or the epicenter, or the water, hurricane or whatever."

"May God be with you, Abraham Benterah. What can I do to help?"

"Show me where Amber Pick is broadcasting from and plan that vacation that I spoke to you about. Or if you like the brutal cold, you can wend your way to Winnipeg in Wescan with us, although thanks to global warming, it apparently is not so bad right now. You are welcome, my friend."

"I will. Amber is conversing with the people through that second door on the right. He ain't going to like this much, but, when you convince him of the true cause, he won't mind so much, I think. He's kind of an asshole."

The Abbie walks toward a door labelled Studio 1 and opens the door.

"Hi, there. Mr. Amber Pick, I presume. I have been an admirer of yours, at least for the last ten to fifteen seconds or thereabouts. I would like to do a zingercast with you today about a subject that will be close to the souls of many of your conversationalists today. The souls in their spirit world, not the ones right under their feet, so to speak. We are going to try to convince the washed and the unwashed, the uncorrupted or the corrupt, the uninitiated or the new initiate, the radical or the conserve, religious righteous, or the non-spiritual or anyone about the importance of coming forward to save themselves and perhaps the coast."

"Break for the commercial. Who the hell are you? Ralph, who is the fucker, and get him out of here. We've only got a minute before we're back zinging into the homes."

"Listen to what he has to say, Mr. Pick."

"I listen to nothing. Get your hand away from me, imbecile. I'll have the network guards throw you out of here. Ralph, don't just stand there praying; get your hand off me, you Abraham! I will be delighted to help you, Abraham. What am I saying!"

"You were saying that you were going to help me on my quest for the wondrous land of Winnipeg. Let's shake hands on this, my loquacious friend and plot macher"

"I will help you, Abraham, but I feel compelled. I don't want to, but I have to."

The Amber holds his hands on his head. This is interesting in that he tried to resist the touch but could not do it. It is not causing a lot of pain.

"What the hell is happening to me?"

"Thank you, Amber. Time is passing. I need to use the Interact to inform the people.

Ladies and gentlemen, uncles and aunts, I give you permission to pull down your pants. That's not what I want to say. I wish to tell you all that mares eat oats and does eat oats and little lambs eat ivy; a kid will eat ivy, too, wouldn't you?

Amber, I'm afraid something is wrong. I can't seem to get out what I want to. I'm not in control. Who the hell is?! Ladies and gentlemen, if you can still hear me and want to make a new start on life, repair civilization, and return to earlier, simpler, biologic lifestyles, join me. We have run off the rails. We must return to the order of the hive, the pack, the human condition if we are to survive. My path eventually is to Winnipeg. Nothing will come easily, but we will have to relearn together. We will have to demonstrate a new direction for mankind. If you do not want to participate in this adventure, the consequences may be severe, but that is your free choice. I believe I also have the choice. Please come with me. My name is Abraham."

"We are no longer on Interact, Abraham. Something happened. I think we went off when you finished about the kid eating ivy. We may have got the path and rails stuff on, I'm not sure. But we're not getting anything else out. I will have to check as to why. Did you say what you wanted to say?"

"No, Amber, not exactly. But it seems that was all I could say. Perhaps that is all I was meant to say. I could not mouth the words of the impending disaster. I was controlled, stopped. I don't understand."

The Amber person jumps up and is forcing his way out of the control room.

"Controlled; what the fuck did I do, anyhow? Why did I let you take over my Interact broadcast? God!"

"Amber, it seems that if God is involved in this, he is an unforgiving God. But why would some other form, some extra-terrestrial, care at all? I don't know what's going on. Perhaps someone is just fed up. Well, I may as well stop talking to myself. This is not productive. Thanks for the cooperation, Amber. I know you felt it deeply. Despite my rights, if the ratings are good, feel free to rebroadcast the program. You can leave the mares to eat oats out if you like. I don't know if that added anything to my message."

"Get the hell out of here, you fool. I don't know what you did to me, but I'll kill you if you try whatever you did again!"

"Amber, your brain patterns must be so messed up that the narcissism just breaks through. Nonetheless, I must tell you that you should take an immediate vacation if you value your existence. I'm not sure where you should go; the Ozarks might be a reasonable place. Well, goodbye, everyone, and thanks for all the hospitality."

"Just get out of here, and take your strangeness with you, fucker!"

"Amber, my friend, how did you become so wise and mature so suddenly? Oh, never mind, I guess I had better get going. I do have a job to do, and I had better get to it. I have totally failed here. Sometimes the boss just doesn't tell you what's going on so you can do the job. In my case, not only has the boss not made things clear, but I don't even know who the boss, or Boss is. It would make things easier for one of little faith like myself. Why me? Ladies and gentlemen, uncles and aunts, I give you permission to pull down your pants! Did I actually say that?! I don't have the magic touch; I'm just tetched. Somebody or something else definitely has the power and is just using me to deliver it.

The Abbie is upset with us. We used him but it is for the good of all. He goes to the doors of the station.

"Goddamn doors. What the hell is wrong with those doors, or me, anyway? It didn't interfere with the Interact, at least for a short while. And then we went off the airwaves. I don't know. I was able to ride the shooter. Nothing happened with that. What's interfering? Well, Abe, if I can address my inner self. I can't think. It's hard to interrogate myself. It's taken me over. Has this happened before to anybody, to humanity? Is this God or some other life form directing our cultural evolution? Well, I may as well play it out. It does have a good ring to it. Am I really going to have a son by Seri without any exogenous slug of progestins and estrogens? If I have a son, should I call him Isaac, or should I break the string and call him Win or Peg? Enough of this! I just have to put my head down and get going."

The Abbie moves out of the station and back to the shooter. He is shaking his head. We have caused him much confusion.

"I have to make sure the family is safe. I have to find out about the people I somehow know about in Chicago, Helen Bette, and Ike. They need to come with us, at least for a bit. They need some direction. Ike is wild, but maybe I can help him somehow. What an upbringing he had! I wonder where that wolf cub is. Is he the leader of the pack with the gift? What gift, and how do I know all these things? Steady, Abe, let's just get going and get as many as we can to safety, or at least to some northern forsaken place in another country. What if there is no quake or disaster? Do we return? Or is the disaster the civilization we have built? Well, it would be interesting to see Wescan, anyhow. See a moody Manitoba morning, a prairie town, and the true flatlands. Maybe the soil of Winnipeg will give me some answers. Perhaps the touch will make things come free. I will continue on this quest, regardless of what happens on our west coast. Let's hit the shooter and get the doggies to move along; you know the banks of the Red will be your new bed."

Merge. It is unfortunate that we had to intervene in the broadcast, but a simple calculation of the probabilities demonstrates that more destruction would occur if the Interact were to proceed as Abraham planned. The path now seems clear.

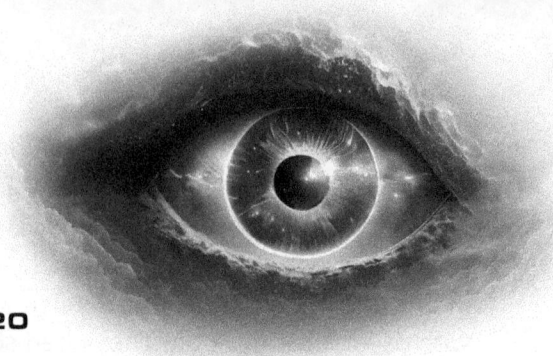

CHAPTER 20

Returns

The Abbie has stopped the shooter and is approaching the group in the shopping center parking lot.

"Hi, everyone. I'm back. I think it's time to move out. Let's forward the wagons; let's roll. Rollin, rollin, keep those doggies rollin . . . rawhide."

"Abbie, I'm glad you're back. We have a problem."

"What do you mean we, white eyes? What's the problem? Where's Lloyd and Gloria, and . . ."

"Gloria and one of the girls wanted to go back to Frisco. I'm not sure whether they just wanted to pick up something they forgot, which is what Gloria said, or whether they just had it with the whole idea of leaving. It's everything they know, and I don't think they could leave without seeing the city again. I tried to stop them, but they were determined. They left without telling Lloyd, who was wandering off somewhere in Sacramento. As soon as I found him, he went after them, but they had quite a start on him."

"For God's sake! Why is she so goddamned stupid! Why doesn't she have any patience? What in the goddamned hell do I have to do to convince people of the danger? Why can't I convince anyone? Why won't it let me save anyone? What the hell is going on anyway? Goddammit, this is frustrating!"

The Seri places her hand on his chest over his heart. It feels pleasant.

"I understand, honey. You've done all you could. It sounds like you weren't all that successful at the Interact. What happened? People thought you were some type of drug-maddened idiot?"

"You know, someone should write a 'how to be a prophet' book with a clear set of instructions. The only thing that I'm not sure of is who I'm a prophet for."

"Abraham, you did what you could. Now tell me about the Interact. It obviously did not go well. With all the disasters that have befallen this area of the world from earthquakes HIV, and Covid, you'd think people would believe you. So, what did you tell them? What were their questions?"

"I told them to pull down their pants and swim like a fish."

"What do you mean, Abraham? Why would you joke at a time like this? Are you kidding me again, or did something go wrong on the Interact?"

"Something happened to me, Sarah. My friend in my head butted in. He or it, or she, I suppose, can be quite the buttinsky. He blocked me from saying anything much except about fish. Anyhow, I didn't create panic in the street. There won't be any worries about millions of people taking to the shooterways and causing power lockups because of the massive reckless driving. Maybe that's why he stopped me from doing that. Maybe he wasn't locking people in so much as saving a few more by stopping other calamities around the major disaster. Maybe he does see more than I do. I dunno the answer."

"Why wouldn't God guide you to help the people in the best way possible?"

"God, or the departed Martian canal people, or whatever, seems to want people to come to their own conclusions or to help themselves. My totally uninspiring talk will have had to be enough. But that's all rationalization because I feel this force should be good, so I'm trying to find good reasons. I really don't know, and it all beats me to hell. Sometime soon, we are going to witness some huge disaster, some colossal darkness. It may not be an earthquake because seismologists do not detect any plate shifting around here. But I understand that we are going to witness, sometime soon, a disaster that will cause the loss of millions of lives. And why and for what purpose? Why would a god or former canal people from Mars or anyone want to destroy all those lives? Maybe he or it can read the disaster and is trying to alert everyone, but then why am I not able to effectively warn anybody? Maybe he wants to destroy the cities as a lesson of some type. But why? What will it prove? What will people take away from that? They may not be the best of cities, but certainly, they can't be the worst. What is it all proving?"

"Abraham, I don't know what for sure it would prove, but it would confirm beyond a shadow of a doubt that there is another force in the world, another influence outside our own, which has a purpose and a direction for humanity. Our civilization has been on the decline for some time. You've said it. The once proud countries of humanity have become warring city-states. Nothing really means anything anymore. There is no right or wrong. There never was right and wrong, of course. There were just shades of grey. At one time, in more primitive societies, the punishment for crime was fierce and cruel. But what was a crime? Was it speaking one's mind, disagreement with the Quran, or an interpretation of the Bible? At that time, few distinguished between the mighty wrong and itty bitty wrong. Now, no one is punished. We must not punish. We must not hurt individual rights, which means that society is punished. Therefore, society has to strike at other societies, other cities towns. We are unable to draw any lines in the sand. Nothing stands for anything anymore! Why have we swung so far? I don't think there is one thing our society can stand for anymore! We can't even hope for our favorite sporting team. The only people who really have goals are those that take things for themselves. And we can't stop them because they, too, have the right."

The Seri is now pacing. Have the Abbie's thoughts penetrated into the Seri? He has not tried to influence her but has often touched her.

"The excitement of the last two centuries has gone. The civilization of those two cities is representative of the deadness, the non-direction of our society. I'm excited, Abbie. Maybe this is really a rebirth for our civilization, a new chance to set things right. Oh, Abbie, we will not only be part of it all, but we will also be leading it."

"I dunno, Seri. I dunno. I do know that I'm a lucky man to have someone like you. You bring brightness and maybe real sense to all this. I wish I could truly believe. It's all so strange. The cause for all of this is not apparent to me."

The Abraham takes Seri in his arms and kisses her.

Something is happening to us. He is pulling us in and integrating us in his brain. What he will do is becoming unknown. Should we stop him? We have to give him the lead. Submerge.

"I wonder if I've got enough time to go after Lloyd and family before the catastrophe. My sense was that we had to leave almost immediately. Wait, is that Lloyd's shooter vehicle? Do you see anyone inside? Is it Lloyd?

Lloyd, is that you? Lloyd, you're as white as a sheet! What happened?"

"Uncle Abbie, it was the most bizarre thing I ever saw. Gloria rented a shooter and just shot back toward San Francisco. The shooter must have been defective. I don't know where she may have gotten it. Something, something happened to it, or some type of weird failure. The shooter left the shooterway. It . . . it's not supposed to happen, is it? Even if they come off the track, they're supposed to brake automatically. But Gloria's didn't. it left the shooterway, rolled, and then righted itself. There appeared to be an electrical arc or something like that, and Gloria and my daughter Mona looked like they were covered in ashes or salt or something like that. They were standing there frozen. I thought they were dead. I went up to them and started wiping off the salt or whatever, and Gloria just stood there. She didn't appear to be dead, but she was cold as a stone. I couldn't talk to them. I couldn't make them talk to me or move them to come back with me. They were just standing, looking back at San Francisco and not moving a muscle. It must have been an electric arc or something which paralyzed them because they were so rigid, but they were awake. I tried to move or drag them over to my shooter, but they were as heavy as stone! I tried to reason but got no response. They're not coming with us. I just don't know what to do."

"Lloyd, my nephew, Gloria and Mona are all right then. At least as all right as they ever are."

"Well, they just stood there, covered in that white ash. They just stood there and stared. They seemed rooted to the spot. But they wouldn't turn around and come back. And they were so heavy, like they were rooted to the ground. It was just weird."

"Gloria's a determined woman. She can take care of herself. As I said before to you a thousand times, you're probably better off without her. I would let her go and do what she has to do. Listen to me, Lloyd, come with us. Whatever Gloria will do, she will do, but it will lead to the moral destruction of you both. Try to pull yourself together, Lloyd, and come with us. We are the wave of the future. Gloria epitomizes the old way."

"It was all so strange, Abbie, so strange. I think I will take the remaining kids and come with you. I feel empty, just empty. I don't know, but I'm following you, Abraham."

The Lloyd looks calmer and more in control of himself than we have seen. It is good he has made a decision to go.

"Lloyd, that 'God be with you,' stuff seems to be gone. That emotional experience must have shocked it out of you. It's rather nice to be speaking to you again, I guess. So what do ya say, Lloyd, are you ready for the journey, the wend, the sally forth, the big excursion? Let's see what the future holds for us. Let's tackle the world and bring it down to our level. Let's gain some control over our future. Whatdiya say, folks, whatdiya say?!"

"I'm not sure what you mean, Abbie. But I do feel it is right to go with you. Maybe it will recapture what's left of this worthless life of mine."

The Lloyd, the Seri and the Abbie, begin walking to their shooter. Many others are arriving now and greeting the Abbie. He waves back at them, and we note he has some joy.

"By the way, Lloyd. Did you have any trouble getting back on the shooterway? No malfunctioning or anything like that? Did you see any problem with anyone else? Also, did you try to pick me up on the Interact?

"The Interact didn't seem to be receiving in the area. Must have been the same thing that interfered with Gloria's shooter. No, that's not right. I came up blank on 2389, but the other channels were working, come to think of it. It seemed to be interference just on the channel you were on. The shooter wasn't acting normally, either. When I tried to have it make the swing turn away from San Fran, it wouldn't go. I had to manually turn it. I even had to push a bit, and then it started up and drove normally."

"Lloyd, Seri, let's get back to the Interact station and see if they can locate any casts from San Francisco. Lloyd, were any of the casts you heard originating from that area?"

"Yeh, some of them were, Abraham. But that was a while ago. Do you think it might have happened already, Abbie?"

"I don't know. I expected to feel something, something in my mind, or the earth to shudder or something. I don't know. I certainly hope not. Maybe there is still a way to convince people to leave. God, you'd think people would believe in catastrophes by now. Earthquakes, famines, floods, pandemics, my god. Enough has happened. This has been mysterious from the beginning. It is as if we were not destined to convince people. Hell, I'm wandering again."

"So, it is a quake you feel coming will hit both those cities?"

"I had a sense of a destructive event of some type. Actually, it feels like a darkness falls over everything. I translated that into a quake because that's what you kinda think of around here. I didn't visualize a quake specifically, though. It could be a tidal wave, I suppose, the one with the Japanese name. Let's see what other massively destructive force. Has Godzilla attacked in the last couple of hundred years? What about another plague? We have had several of those. Hey, here's the Interact station."

"Did you see death and destruction, Abbie?"

"Lloyd, maybe you haven't changed as much as I thought. No, nothing particularly gory. It was more a sense of immediate impending doom and a sort of feeling that you had to get the hell out of there. It was a dying civilization, turning in on itself. Maybe it was what Seri was talking about before. Maybe we just had to leave, or we'd be eaten by the same rot or the monster of civilization or something."

We must leave before we are incorporated. We do not wish to develop some new lifeform. We have done all we could do. We will have to let it develop as it will. Goodbye, Abbie

"Abraham, Abbie, what's happening? Are you having a stroke? You are frozen."

"Huh? Yeh, I'm okay, I think. I feel a little funny but okay. Actually, I feel different, but okay."

"So, you think Gloria and Mona will be okay?"

"Well, I hope so, Lloyd. I don't see anything individually. But what I experienced was a sense of doom. Here's the Interact station. Let's go in and find out what we can find out. Oops, what the hell!'

"Abraham, what's wrong? You're staring at the door. It's just a door. What do you see?"

"You're damn right I'm staring. Did you see what happened?"

"We walked up, the doors opened, and you stopped dead in your tracks."

"I stopped dead because the doors opened! I almost forgot what it was like to walk up to one of those doors and have it open for me. I don't know if my friend, inside my head, is with me anymore! My memories and the knowledge I have of Helen is still there, but I do feel different. Let's go in and see if anything else is changed."

Ms. Rosa, I'm back. May I speak to Ralph or Amber? Are they still around?"

"Yes, Abraham. They're upstairs' you know where. Apparently, something's happened to all the Interact stations broadcasts from San Francisco and L.A."

"Okay. We're on our way up. Dammit, I thought there still was a little time. Here we are. Ralph, Amber, what's up?"

"Abraham, you're back! You were right. Something has happened to all the communication from L.A. and San Francisco. We're trying to raise someone to find out what's going on. Wait, there's a report now coming in from a Zeppelin flyer who apparently was trying to land in L.A. The aeroports were all dark, with no communications of any type. He spotted some people setting fires on the aerostrip to light the way. They weren't even using the emergency flashers; he didn't know why. There must have been some type of massive power failure. The entire city is dark. No sign of Emats or car lights on the old freeways, no lights on the shooterways, no lights anywhere, except for fires. Just nothing!"

"People . . . did he say that he saw people moving about?'

"Wait, I'm just catching another cast from the Zeppelin. Yep, he can see fires on the landing strips and people scuttling around between them. He's also seen people getting out of their shooters on the shooterways. There are pileups on the shooterways. I have never heard anything like it. Those shooterways were perfect. They eliminated human error in travel. Why, no accidents have ever happened! How could this happen?! Some type of terrorist attack? It must have been something like that. Anyhow, there are lots of people milling around."

"So, there was no earthquake, no hurricane, no tsunami, no big dramatic event. Somebody just turned off all the power, and I mean all the power. No terrorist group would have the know-how to do that. They are such small, disconnected groups. But lack of power is to be catastrophic! How can you live? The city is black. There are no ways to communicate, no way to travel except on foot; all energized fences are inactive. Think of the looting. Most weapons based on energy will not work. It will be complete anarchy!"

"Yeh, it may be way more than the lights. Think of it. No energy to the entire area. Wait, there is more coming in. Yeh, the same thing seems to be happening in Frisco. All sorts of people running around there, too. Shit, there must be thousands caught on elevators, undergrounds, shooters going out of control. Food will rot in refrigerators, and people can't pump water. What about all the respirators in hospitals and all the other electrical stuff? They're all supposed to have backup units, but they didn't seem to work for the landing strips. The cities are going to be disasters, a complete shemozzle! I don't think the earthquakes caused as much disaster. How do we get in there without electrical power? We'll have to use wind or something. Certainly, we should not resurrect internal combustion engines. The zeppelins are even reporting trouble with their electrical systems until they clear the area. How are they going to send in rescue units? What the fuck caused all this? What were you saying was going to cause this, Abraham? You knew it was coming."

"I knew something was coming, Amber, but I didn't know what or exactly when. As to what caused it, I'm not sure. My bet is that there was either some type of energy drain or enormous power surge. As to what or who might have caused it, your guess is probably as good as mine. If the energy was drained away, where did it go? Was this extraterrestrial? I was trying to avert something, but I did not even know would happen. I just wanted people to clear out! There is bound to be someone who remembers my attempts at warnings and blames me, but I don't have the expertise to make this catastrophe happen! I don't think anyone does. How many people will be hurt? How many? How could it have been avoided, how?"

"But I had help regarding my prescience. Someone or something knew about this, this thing, and was trying to direct me. I don't know who or what. Was it God? Was this an extraterrestrial? I don't know. Will it spread? Are we going back to the stone age? No communication, transportation, food supply, what will happen?

Old Abe here stopping my streaming for the moment. I can see them all looking at each other. No power, no internet, and companies' records are gone. It was the mother of all catastrophes.

"Well, Abbie. They'll have to figure out the cause to find out how to avoid it spreading. They'll probably be writing about this for the next 98 years. Some type of chain reaction must have picked off all the power stations and generators, even if they weren't connected. Anything electrical or associated with power stations appears to be hit. Boy, I think we can call this the Big Blackout. I wonder if anyone else knows about it yet? We could report it before anyone. The Big Blackout!"

"Amber, Ralph, I think you will be the first to report the Blackout. Perhaps, you can even tally or guess on the tragedies that are occurring. Keep with it; the rest of the world should know. You've got quite a story here. Hey, I even know an angle. Tell them maybe God did it because you can't explain it any other way. Tell them there was a messenger around predicting this. God did it because he is starting to take some stock accounting down here. That should really carry the story."

"Yeh, an act of the Supreme being! He turned out the lights, the Blackout. Hey, maybe he turned out the lights and left town. Yeh. Abraham, you were predicting something would happen, although you didn't exactly hit the nail on the head."

"No, you're right. I didn't hit the nail on the head. I deserve credit for nothing. I deserve credit for not being able to get people to change or leave. I pulled out my family and a few others. It was a magnificent job I did. No, you don't have to give me credit for anything. There are always some people predicting disaster; somebody's bound to be right sometime. It's your story for sure."

"Great, let's get on to the Interact before anyone else comes in with this story. The Big Blackout hits the big two west coast cities. Thousands, no, what am I talking about!?! Millions left stranded, hospitals paralyzed, no transportation, and we can't seem to get in. It's back to primitive times in the most advanced cities in California. Wow, what a story."

"Abraham, this is terrible. How will the people survive without access to food or water? Violence will break out. How can we help them?"

"I don't think we can, Seri. I do feel that we should strike out and try to provide a better area for our children and even our children's children. They'll be sorting this thing out for years. Maybe the power will come back on and everything or most everything will be set right. I don't know. The cities could empty and disappear unless they can resurrect the power supply in some way. At the moment, though, people can't seem to get in or get out. Think of the blow to the crime families. Unbelievable! The challenge to the civilization of those cities is much worse than an earthquake would have been. Those cities will be reduced to hamlets if the power doesn't come on pretty soon. They'll disappear, covered up by the shifting sands of the Mojave. Well, that may be a little poetic, but I think they may disappear. I wonder what history will say about all that."

"Abraham, all those people. There must be something we can do. We can't leave them there."

"I wish we could do something, Seri, but I don't think we can. We can't seem to get in, and I don't know how we could get people out. There will be some organized rescue attempts, but you know how disorganized things are now, and there won't be a great financial imperative. Most of the credits that ran the cities were local. People in the cities will mobilize and start making their way out. Probably shooters will work on the outskirts and can take people from there. If it spreads, they will have to walk, but some will make it out and tell the story. I don't think our presence will make any difference. No, we must strike out on our own. We must experience our own history. We have things to do and places to see. See you in the funny papers, fellows. I am sure that is a reference you will not understand. Let's go, Seri. Amber is after us. I guess we will have to speak to him."

"Wait, Abraham. I think I want an interview with the man that predicted the disaster, the Big Blackout. Human suffering! This is a great story. And there's an even better twist to the story. That is your twist, Abraham. This was a prophecy from God, right?"

"I can tell how difficult this tragedy is for you, but, of course, it's your duty to report."

"Well, never mind. Prophecy was certainly not one of my strengths. I've never even won a lottery ticket. I was just wandering in the desert. I don't really know how I knew something was coming. I have not actually figured it out, I don't know. Let's just say a little bee told me."

"Wait, how did the prescience come to you? Was it a visual, lights, or sound, booming voice? How would you describe the feeling?"

"Well, Amber, I woke up one morning, and I just wasn't myself. Have you ever had one of those days?"

"So, because you were feeling ill, you divined that something was going to happen on a grander scale. You felt you were like a divining light. Your ill feeling was your sympathetic response to what was going to happen. This must have happened to you before; when you felt that ill in the past other things must have happened. This past experience assured you that something was going to happen, and since you felt so sick, it was going to be severe."

"You know, when I think about it, I couldn't have expressed it better myself, Amber. I really never realized how insightful the newsmakers really were. See you, bye, bye."

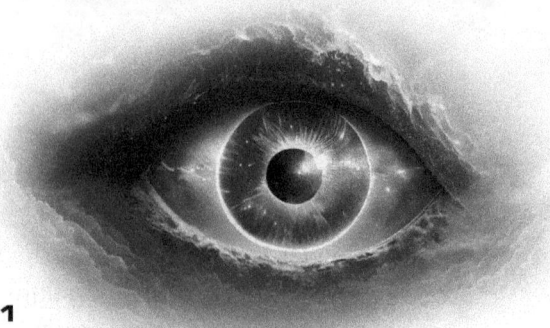

CHAPTER 21

To Unwend Or Rewend

"Well, group, here's the story. Once upon a time, there was this man called Abram, and he had his name changed to Abraham because God gave him the letter from his name, and then . . ."

"Abraham, get serious. What's going on? We are still at the Interact. Where do we go now? What do we do now? We have no home to go back to. We are nomads."

"We are nomads. We will move like shepherds. We will move slowly to Winnipeg in Wescan. We will work along the way and perhaps others will come with us. We have to go to the Chicago area and see about Helen and Ike. We will settle in Winnipeg and rebuild. The future is there for us, for now."

"You were right about something happening. It is amazing! What did happen, and really how did you know?"

"It appears that there has been some type of massive power failure in L.A. and San Francisco, and people are running around unable to move about, unable to leave their immediate neighborhoods, unable to communicate, probably not aware of the enormity of the problem, nor aware of the restricted localities. Everything is at a standstill. It will take a long time to stabilize and rebuild if they can. On the upside, with one stroke, any pollution in the area will be solved. But there will be fighting; millions will die. A new civilization will emerge, and certainly, they will return to some basic values. They will have to. After all the rifts and tribal fighting in the world, and especially in those city-states, perhaps they will emerge stronger, better.

Our path, as I see it, does not lie in that direction because, in some way, we have to stand passively by and wait for people to work their way out. The only way into L.A. and San Fran would be on horseback or in a covered wagon. I'm fresh out of wagon trains right now. No, I see us now setting out to Chicago. I expect to hang around there for a while because Seri is pregnant, as many of you know. I don't know if the same problems befell Chicago. It could have. We will see. By the time we reach Chicago with the entire entourage, Seri will probably be ready to give birth. I know it will not be a record birth for someone her age but going through menopause at 52 and without the help of implantations, or hormonal manipulation, it must be up there. Anyway, there are some people there I wish to meet, Helen Bette and young Ike. From there, I plan to wend our way to Winnipeg with Helen, Ike, and Redass, or whatever we call the baby. I hope all of you will come with me."

"Of course, we will, Abbie. I think everyone realizes there is nothing to return to in L.A. or San Francisco. Years ago, I set my path to walk with you, and I certainly will continue to stand by you, honey. So, for me, so be it. Chicago and Winnipeg will be our goals. I can't say I feel completely content about the people you are determined to find, but for all I know, with your record, who knows, it will be interesting, even if they don't exist.

But there is absolutely no way we are going to name our little miracle, Redass. Are you even thinking of trying to name the baby after that wolf you mentioned?"

"Helen and Ike or Ian are real. I know that for a fact. I have a complete memory of them, and a real feeling for them, although I've never met them. Redass, of course, is our son. But that's my little joke to myself. It's not after any wolf; they have no names. Winnipeg was built on the path of the fur trade route, which travelled on the Red and Assiniboine Rivers. It is built on the junction of those two rivers, and there is a trading area built there at 'the Forks.' Since we are going to the junction, our son should be named after the two rivers, Redass, no?"

"In a word, NO. Abraham, there are limits to our interwoven path, as I mentioned before, and this is one of the areas are paths unwend, so to speak. Redass will not be the name of our son. I'm not going through all this for a Redass. We will pick another name for the child. How do you know it will be a son? We haven't checked that out yet, remember?"

"I would be happy with a daughter or son. But I know it is a boy, just like I knew you were pregnant. Okay, so a son. What should we name him? Let's not name him Isaac. We could name him anything else but Isaac or Winnie. It mustn't be Winnie. Winnie was a real bear and then he became a storybook by A. A. Milne. In the book, he became a stuffed bear, and there he remains. We can't name him that."

"Abraham, don't be so silly. I was thinking something like Manly, after my father, may his soul rest in peace."

"Manly, Man, come on, Man, yeh, that's good. In Hebrew, that would probably be Moshe. Now he led the people out of Egypt. Joseph led them there. I recognize that this rings like the story from the Bible. It doesn't follow exactly, but there sure are similarities. So, when we have a son, we can change the story. His name doesn't have to be Isaac. We're not going to Israel, so our future and experiences will be different. We don't have to repeat history or the Bible, do we?

I hope that all the people in those two cities survived. Many, perhaps most will find their way out. Just the cities were destroyed, not all the people. Please, not all the people."

"It's all right, Abraham. I know why you get silly. When the pressure builds, then you vent by making some silly joke. I wonder whether the Abraham from the Bible had a silly sense of humor. Abbie, you did what you could, honey. Now we must build a new life for all of us and for our son."

"When should we start out, Uncle? We are still at the Interact parking lot. I've decided not to go back and try to find Gloria. She'll prosper somehow from all of this. Gloria is a survivor. She won't be happy becoming a nomad."

"Now is as good a time as any to get going, Lloyd. I think you've made the right decision about Mona and Gloria. It was time for a parting of the ways."

"I think if there was anything left between Gloria and me, it's gone now, Abraham. Perhaps she'll decide to follow me later if we make out really well. We can try to work that out. I'm very close to the two girls; they'll accompany us. I'd appreciate Seri's input with them. You know how teenage girls are. Like all kids, they are going through their strange teenage years, but I think they'll settle down, especially with Seri's help."

"Remember, Lloyd; we don't have to repeat the same biblical story. The girls are at an impressionable age. Remember the biblical story and watch yourself with them. Gloria was not the best mother in the world, and morality is something that simply is not taught anymore. They will be a handful, but don't take me literally."

"So, are we going now, Abraham? Let's get on with it."

"We're rolling, or rather shooting on the shooter, folks. It's Chicago or bust. Seri, you know I'm going to have to teach our son baseball?"

"Abraham, you will. You'll probably want to teach him all those crazy games people used to play."

"Well, baseball in particular. You know, we could name him Yogi. Yogi, he was a great philosopher and baseball player. And I guess Yogi is a little like Yitzhak or Isaac. I'll have to teach him how to sacrifice . . ."

"Look, Abbie, my dear. It looks like thunder is in the distance, but the storm is going the other way. We should have clear sailing."

THE END OF THE BEGINNING

Printed in the USA
CPSIA information can be obtained
at www.ICGtesting.com
LVHW050321310823
756310LV00001B/1

9 780228 892625